MIDDLEWATCH SUSAN KERSLAKE

The crimson geranium. Fretted edges casting shadow pools on the softer colour of petals beneath. Dew-fed in the window-box. Apart and shining in the dumb confused cabin that says so much to him and nothing to her. It is hot in the one room now, but the sweat on the wood walls is the remnant of night cold, melted frost in the middle of summer.

The girl is alone, a heap of sand, an island barely breathing life. In the middle of this chaos, discarded, she lies on a blanket and straw mattress. The window is broken, its curtain snatched down, now strangling on a corner nail. Bare walls, shelves swept naked, broken cups, bent plates, extra utensils, spoons, knives splattered amid dirt and ashes. The table in the centre of the room has a silent sharp knife embedded in it. The chairs are tossed back. A trunk, moss hidden in its leather hinges, brass points of wear, olive green. Its humped top thrown open leaning into a dent in the wall. All the lavender is lost in the open air; it lies like dried-out rice among the torn clothes. All rags now, pieces of fringe and drawn-thread work, careful embroidery shredded and strewn until no colour is left whole, nothing belongs to what it was. The ruins of a dead fire; ashes creeping under the wind, softly breathed out in a film from the stone-cold fireplace. The kindling is all gone, the logs are in a heap. They too are steaming.

There is a fall of sun coming in the door, moving, perceptible in the ashen air. As it reaches the bed in the afternoon there is a flutter of the girl's flesh. Air stirs, new air, shuffling the debris, moving in the room as winds do in deserted places, bringing in the wandering flies, letting them out again. Carpenter ants climbing over the wooden stoop. The mice inspecting corners and next spring birds may nest inside.

Now the girl is breathing the sunshine, her tongue comes out of her mouth to feel it; it does this without touching her lips, as if they are stung and painful.

5

The man shuts the sun out with his body, standing beside the bed. She does not move unless the colour of her skin so exposed seems to falter. Then her hands lying half-open, small cups broken, begin to tremble. He loses the trembling under the ground of her flesh. Then it reappears. Her eyelids. Her eyes are open, wide, uncommonly wide, as if in total darkness or trying to encompass a new shadow. Only shadow, not shape, not colour, not his substance, not the brown cord pants, the pale blue shirt wrinkled on his arms, open at the throat for the heat. He yanks the curtain from its nail and though she is all alone somewhere, he covers her nakedness, her hands like dried leaves, curled, her hip bones: the roots of trees sprung out of the ground; her thighs curdled black and blue, welt and bruise. His fingers smooth and fumble at her torn smock, finding a shred of tie to knot at her breast, to cover the bird-cage bones, the prints of some sort of blows, animal prints running on the bridges of her ribs. Still she does not move, acknowledge him.

"Sibbi," said to wake gently, but wake all her body. "Sibbi!"

Her eyes waver for a moment, then snap shut. The name is. The crimson asserts itself under her eyelids where none can see it, anoints the inside of her head, as if someone were calling her name, gently, and it turned into colour. She twinges because it is so ravenous. It bites; sparks hot from the striking anvil light in her blood until the pain races down her skin. He pushes the wisps of hair out of her face and she shudders, but the two are not related as he thinks: she in response to his touch. Rather she is fleeing the ravages of blood, her blood.

Then inert again as he sits her up. She remains there, eyes open again and vacant. He moves to the end of the bed, first to one post and then to the other, cutting the rope knots tied first to her ankles, then around the posts. It has worn

6

not at all in the wood, but around her ankles, drained white and cold, are raw snakes, burned beneath the bleached skin, down to where there is still blood. She doesn't seem to watch or feel his hands around her bones, trying gently to put her legs together. Her feet are filthy in his soiled hands.

He feels a chill as if from the pit of a mine, the black damp cold from the coal shaft. It comes in a wave, sudden and sharp. In its wake the wonder of the world in its shape, birth or death, but neither, the wail, the flaying of a sound in the air. Its fall like chaff, a wing in a spider's web. The smoke and ashes of her thighs as she plucks the curtain up her legs. The mud colour of blanket and flesh, the same. Her fingers open like feathers, float above, hover over the weeping stone of her skin.

Her hands sway, with them her body; slightly, this way then that way, then silent and quiet. She is vacant, still and cold. A shape, and she clings to it because if she does not nothing will come near her again.

The sun is stretching long, lean in the calm, in the heat of early evening. The flowers are beginning to close up, giving back to the earth its own colour. Drying all day, the dust billows away from footfalls as cows and men make their way home. The silence of caravans, of the day shift returning and the night creatures not out yet.

"It's time to go home," he says. "And since she's no home to go to, she'll come to mine." He cannot forget her naked, tied, and left in offering to the night. He'll give her a roof and cover against the aimless dark.

One day in the wind, one day alone and the grasses will begin to grow across the path; no longer swished aside, the long blades will lean farther, until miniature haystacks slide into the gut of human paths. The cabin is left on the hill; the hill is left to the waving seasons.

He carries her, hoping the motion doesn't hurt her. She gives no sign, no sigh. In her head the hurting, the confusion. She is holding an arm; she knew whose it was, but can't remember. The motion is soothing, the sound of boots settling into the dry grass of the bluff. She doesn't dare open her eyes; then she can't.

This man, Morgan, stopped on his way home to pick up Mrs. Clery: midwife, mother, maker of home medicinal brews. She appeared squinting into the setting sun, wiping her perpetually wet hands on her apron. One hand up to shade her eyes, to see the limp form in Morgan's arms.

"What!" she peered at the crust on the eyes and lips.

"Would you come and clean her up?" asked Morgan, feeling her bare flesh timidly in his hands, now that they had company.

"It's Sibbi, isn't it?" Curiosity swept over her face. Curiosity more than concern. "What's she got into?" Without answer she continued, "Yes, let me finish up here." She turned to one of her own numerous children, smushing him back into the white kitchen. The door shut abruptly.

Morgan shifted the hollow burden slightly, getting hold of some dry skin. Hill and rock settled gently in the soft wind and pinking sky. Morgan walked on the weed hummock between the dry rocky ruts. The summer evening stretched, grass rippled like fur along a cat's back.

Morgan had come from the city to teach here, in the old wood-and-stone building at the end of the road. Beyond there was nothing but the raw land stopped by the sea. He liked being on the edge: able to walk out the back door and see not a thing built by man; out the front door and know the road ran down into the village where people lived and breathed. The village bare, huddled close together, fenced for security. Painted houses, and in the curve of the harbour mirroring the colours, the boats. At this hour safe home like all the people, shuttering in for the night.

Morgan had been here long enough to have had this child in his arms in his classes. Coming down when her brother let her, or the weather let her, or her own will let her. Coming down through the pine trees, smelling of sheep and pine pitch, softly like a wisp of smoke, the starting of a fire in the woods. There was no way to make her come against the will of all those things. Who would fetch her from the surly scowl of her brother who stood in the door of their shack, his legs apart to the edges of the frame, one arm stretched across the opening? And where was Sibbi? With the flock in the hills, who knows where. No-one would go up when the snow lay so deep, the land was smoothed in snowhills, or when the rain soaked the hollows to a sodden marsh. And no-one could catch the silent will-o'-the-wisp when she was free, waving like wheat.

She came first on a grey moist day which was Saturday and stood, bare feet on the floor, arms out like the ears of a mouse. Her eyes busy in the empty room. In her muslin she became another shaft of grey-white light. Morgan came in from outside with the broom, stifled his surprise to say calmly, every day:

"Hello Sibbi," and turned away from her to walk the broom to its corner. "Today is Saturday, no kids, but you can stay if you like." Still not looking at her, as one does with an animal, averting the eye, getting it used to the voice. "You know where the books are, or if you would like to draw. . . ?" She could see the broom was properly in its place and he would have to turn.

Instead he went around the desks and benches to the open door of his room. Sibbi walked up the aisle and when he was gone she took his place at the lectern, barely able to see over it. A hand at each corner. She stood like the figurehead on the prow of a ship. Morgan was walking around his room; she heard him settle into a chair, then the radio went on. The schoolroom filled with music. Sibbi put her hand to her forehead, held her hair out of the way. She climbed down from the lectern and walked to the back of the room. She

9

didn't like anyone to get behind her. She sat on the empty corner of the last bench and folded her hands on the desk. The bleating of sheep and the ugly noises of her brother were far away. She remained so still for so long that Morgan began to fear for her. He put his book down and rose to the door. Sibbi started up. He said quickly:

"Would you like a piece of bread? I'm hungry, aren't you?" He felt he could invite her specially, she was apart from the other children, like a gypsy. "Forlorn," someone had said once, thinking about her, and the lean of her body when around people. "Vagabond," not said kindly by mothers who feared the wings of their own children.

Sibbi would have no bread today. A polite shadow, restrained, constricted, she slid off her bench and walked toward the door.

"Sibbi!" She actually halted there on the threshold, symbolically, Morgan thought, one foot in each world. "Sibbi, you will come back again—" as a gentle reminder.

But the days grew longer in the sun, to their apex. And the days grew shorter as the sun swung shy each day. And all the time Sibbi was hidden in the deepening expanse of green. Sometimes she was seen in grass up to her knees, that hand held across her brow, still as a post, brown and weathered. At other times she crouched in the grass up to her armpits, elbows akimbo with a joint of hay under her tongue. Morgan waved at her stony little figure. She never waved back.

Morgan arrived back from the city just in time for the beginning of school. On the first day they all sat there trapped brown and tousled. All too soon the leaves lost their freedom and fell to the earth, and the children settled into their desks day after day. Morgan tried to keep their eyes bright though their bodies grew pale. When he went into town there was little talk of the children and little to talk to him about. He listened obediently and knew enough.

Once his habits had been learned and everyone knew them, they said, "He's quiet I'll say, but the children seem to like him." The summing up.

And no Sibbi. Staying out of reach of the other children. Just too far to make it worth their while to chase her. Besides they'd seen her brother when he came to town; rattling down out of the hills behind the ragged pony and the two-wheeled cart full of bags of wool, or a few sheep brought down to be slaughtered. His dog had a better look in his eye than Jason. Jason was young and strong; he had come over the hills like a fierce young eagle with his sheep, a dog, a dun-coloured pony, the cart piled high and looking to lose its load with each lurch. And Sibbi, a tiny urchin the women tried to gather up then and there. But they were not allowed and since she always looked to her brother first before doing anything, they gave up trying to get through her dumb stare. Jason was just not comfortable near the village and with each inch that Sibbi grew they withdrew farther up into the hills. "Well, they're not harming, and he keeps the sheep out of trouble." They lived on the horizon, in the bank of fog that so often waited just off the coast from mid-morning to dusk. When Jason came into town he did his business but did not stop to be sociable. When Jason came into town everyone was curious to catch a look in his eyes and everyone was extra civil.

In the last few months of the winter and spring, people began to notice the fog building up around Jason's eyes. His eyes hunting like the inky pools of a snake one moment, the next bewildered, distracted.

One spring day, with patches of snow on the ground and a warm sun in the sky, Jason brought the cart down empty, but very few people noticed, for with him in tow was Sibbi. Her dress was too short, her sweater tattered, frayed at the cuffs, worn out at the elbow. When they stopped she stood and held onto herself by the elbows. Sibbi was growing up, not only out of her clothes, but between her arms she cradled two small breasts. There were no children to stare at her, only the little ones and the adults, who were discreet. Jason went into the store and left her. Sibbi turned her back to the cart, leaned against it. The sky rolled clouds over the sun. Sibbi sank as the street turned grey, the snow hardened in its patches. She was more comfortable now that she did not cast a shadow, that extra dimension of herself, on the ground. In the street here, she only wanted to escape back to the hills; in the hills she yearned sometimes, or wondered what it would be like to belong to this street, curving around the contour of the harbour. To one of the painted houses, white with green trim, flowered curtains imprisoned behind glass windows, homes with the full family safe inside. Jason's dog came and sat beside her on a dry spot and leaned against her skirt. The street was deeply pitted. Mud beginning to form in gouges. The dog was still, but for his nose which he held in the air, toward the store, casting for new smells. Sibbi chewed her lower lip until the chapped places cracked and bled.

Morgan came into town the next day for supplies and more information than he had heard from the children. The day was harsh with drying winds, and bright. The news was still fresh.

"Ah, he was in, took us to the window to see her like she's a new spring lamb of his and wanted to know, could we make the gypsies in the hills move on; imagine, as if all the hills was his to roam. Now the gypsies're no harm, they don't stay long and bring a little colour, a little fortune-telling, trade a few horses and sell our women a shawl with a fringe. He's not minded them before—what would they want with his waxy sister? It isn't true they steal children and she's a child no-more, Mr. Morgan. A pretty little thing, mind, but not a bit of a proper girl anybody'd want, d'you think. . . ?"

But Morgan remembered her, folded hands and flaxen hair, catching the music in his schoolroom, and when she had actually come to a whole day of classes, the way her eyes opened into a mind that was also open, perhaps even eager. The days she'd come he had weighed his words as if it were important she hear something to take away with her; for she had come as something separate, somehow equal; had come because she wanted to come. And had come back, not often to be sure, but she had returned. The anticipation of her visits, unexpected, uncharted, made him stay alert. He thought she was surely drawn to him as a teacher, as a guide to a wider world. When she came it wasn't like the other children, up the road, all in a warm bunch; it was alone, like a pilgrim, down to the only place near the village she felt safe, her place in the back corner, next to the window where it was often cold, but next to the door and her own world.

He left a scribbler and a pencil that she wouldn't touch for a long time. Then one day while he was reading a story to the class she filled in all the little holes in the letters on the cover. The next time she left the pencil sharp and her eyes travelled here and there, to the fire in the black stove showing an orange flame, the heat making the door jiggle, to the maps and pictures on the cracked stained walls, to the books on the shelves. She saw his face, not directly into the eyes, not yet, but his lips, until he felt as if his mouth were full of marbles.

Morgan looked over the class each day, children who wanted to be nameless, for whom these hours did nothing in the outside world, where boys were going fishing with their fathers, and girls learning to mend weather-coats and slickers so the sea could not freeze their men; learning to keep a house together, to make a home. Who among these children would wander into a place where they would want a book in the evening instead of the relief of sleep for a worn-out body? In the meantime, the sums to do, the reading. The words to speak and read, to keep the accounts necessary for this life in the curve of the sea, in the dominion of the season.

Sibbi learned all the letters inside her head and practised them outside with a stick in the dust of her front yard. She learned them big and small and wrote words her brother read to her before they blew away. For Jason knew how to read and write.

In the peace of a golden Indian summer's day before school was open and while Morgan was away for the afternoon, Sibbi went in to her desk and wrote with the sharp pointed pencil on the first page of the scribbler. She printed: "Jason. Dog. Sheep. Tree. Hill." She left a space. Then she printed: "Sibbi. I am Sibbi. Sibbi. Sibbi. . . ."

She got up and walked all round the edge of the room in the shadowed stillness. So light on her bare feet the boards made no sound. She touched the outline of countries on the maps, the colours on the paintings, the cloth spines of the books, and her fingers crept across the tops of the books to see how thick with pages they were. She pressed her hand on the blackboard, then again and again, her moist palm leaving prints. Flies buzzed through the aisles of desks. Sibbi lifted her tassel-coloured hair off her hot neck and let it fall down her back. She stood and folded her hands, ran one over the other the way water washes a pebble in a stream. She was out of her place, had never seen the room from this angle before and was uneasy. Her hands opened, the palms wrung across each other; then they formed a circle, holding an invisible ball, hovering, circling until they came to rest at her throat. She had stayed so long the room was getting quite dark and she had a long way to go.

Morgan came home to the forgotten, open pages, the white paper in a brown dusk. "Sibbi!" The call fell in the dead air. He went to the scribbler there on the desk like a still moth. He read what she had printed so neatly. He sat on the desk top and picked up the paper, trying to figure out what it was that made him want to tame her, to teach her, to lead her out of those brooding hills, away from the sheep. What was it in those cornflower blue eyes, those gestures in the hills, and now, these few properly, carefully printed words on a piece of paper like a million others? Why had she put the words above, like a cloud over an empty space before the small, assertive bundle of her name?

That winter Sibbi came to school even less and seemed more desperate each time. Sometimes she wrote feverishly, only to tear the page out when all the other children had left, crumple it up and throw it into the fire.

"Sibbi, why don't you let me read what you write?" Morgan could not help himself asking. He shouldn't have; it was her private thing to do, as his own words were his, and he would resent the wrong person asking him to expose them when he was trying them out, seeing what they looked like once they were removed from his head. She clenched the papers, her fingers, thin now, like talons and up came those fierce, frightened eyes. "I don't look, Sibbi, but if you ever want me to. . . ," which was a lie; he looked after every visit, but she believed him, she thought; besides there was nothing written there for anyone to see, not in her whole life. Hand to hair, a sign, then she left.

He saw her in the snow that winter, in a gypsy shawl of warm wool. He saw her riding a horse, black as pitch in the white hills, but Jason still came down with the old dun pony. When she wandered into school in the rising of the year he saw in the set of her lips a different kind of knowledge and she seemed to sit more surely in her seat. As if her centre of gravity had shifted; as if her pit was no longer where her quick heart beat, but had sunk to her womb. Her body flowed now, was no longer driven about like the weeds.

Morgan held that body now. It was as if something had to kill her before she could be either captured or saved. He had found her, but only after she had been trapped and tied. The sky was blue and transparent, the skyline of trees turning from dark green to black, the sound of waves on restless stone. He hurried into his house to light the lamps. He laid her on the rug-covered cot in the kitchen where the children lay if they were sick. She was shivering now, indoors, so he covered her with a quilt the women had made him because he seemed to have come with so few of the things that mattered. He built a fire in the stove and lit the kerosene lamp above the cot. Exhausted suddenly and with nothing to do, he sat down. His hands went tensely to his knees. He got up and put kettles of water on to boil. He sat down again. Waited. His eyes hovered over the deathly quiet form under the quilt.

Sibbi did not make one conscious move. When Mrs. Clery came, she propped Sibbi up on a wood chair and washed her vigorously to get the accumulation of ash and dirt off and to try to restore some colour by rubbing. She prodded and peered at every inch of her.

"She's fit," Mrs. Clery pronounced, her hands holding Sibbi's head up, as if she had just delivered her, which indeed she had. "Physically, that is; nothing broken; but she's been beat up pretty bad, y'know." She looked at Morgan after they had put Sibbi back on the cot and covered her.

"I saw Jason," Morgan began, "a couple of days ago, coming down out of the woods with the pony cart full. I didn't think much of it, who ever knows what his comings and goings are? But he never came back. The bluff was so quiet, well, I thought, that's just summer. But when I was in town today and no-one said anything about Jason's visit, well, I was uneasy. And the crows were up there, circling like vultures, screaming and carrying on; I just got curious and, and went up. . . ."

"Did he do that to her, that brother, did he beat her up like that, and chop off her hair then?"

"I guess, who else would've been there?"

"Ah. . . well, Mr. Morgan, what'll become of her now?"

Morgan looked very deliberately into the brown coffee eyes and pink cheeks. "I think I'll keep her here with me." And Mrs. Clery rocked, said nothing, thinking he was, as she said later, "some kind of foolish." "I mean, no-one would have her; if Jason doesn't come back and it looks as if he was escaping now, where'd she go but to the county asylum? Can you see her there?"

"Well of course you know her better than I do. . . ."

"Yes, I do." He believed that.

"She's a child really."

"This is the only place she's ever come to, on her own; she's afraid of the village; she was afraid of Jason yet tied to him, leashed to him, and when she came here I felt, well, somehow as if she was asking me to, not actually do something, but just be here."

"But to keep her here, you being a bachelor and she being, well, out of the ordinary for a child somehow." She didn't know which was predominant.

"Perhaps all the more reason. I'll think I'll try, Mrs. Clery; I can just try, don't you think?"

"Ah, whatever you like; it's certainly a charitable thing to do if you're so disposed." And she sat and rocked a bit and thought about things before packing up her satchel and lighting her lantern to go home.

At the door stoop, "Oh, Mrs. Clery, everything was destroyed up there, d'you know where I could get some clothes for her?"

She looked at him startled. Lives and property both, she thought. "Ah, yes, I'll get you a bundle together."

"Thank you, thank you for everything. You don't think it's too foolish?"

"Oh well, you try, Mr. Morgan. She can go anytime, Jason may come back for her yet. You'll not be bound to her, you know. Welcome and good night then." The night swallowed her.

The night peered in the bare windows on the small kitchen: the black stove, steady lamplight, halos around the chimneys. Pump and sink with dirty plates and cups, a loaf on a plate, potatoes in a burlap sack. A handful of towels on a hook. A plain wooden table with remains of tea, the children's copy books pushed to one side. The walls were a nondescript faded colour, making the whole room look old. Smudge spots on the ceiling. Morgan preferred the soft kerosene lamps to the electric light. He washed his face and hands and inspected the soup pot. He was very tired but also very hungry. The smell of the soup took some of the chill out of his spine. As he ate it with a thick piece of soft white bread the ugly taste in his mouth disappeared. He ate propped up on his elbows looking over his fists now and again to the cot. Sibbi was very still, in a deep sleep beneath her inferno, beneath dreams.

Morgan turned out all but one of the lamps, put more wood in the stove and pulled a blanket over himself in the deep soft chair in the corner. He would sit up with her tonight, in case she woke. He wondered fleetingly what the reaction would be to his *adoption*; he was on a quiet and independent footing here; he didn't feel they would mind, but would find it curious. As he did himself, a peculiar tension of spirit he felt toward the girl. He hadn't been caught by her in a moment, not knowing what or where exactly, only that the river of his life had been diverted from underneath like a beaver building a dam to curb the current. Suddenly one day he was stopped. She was in the way. She had somehow flung light like a cold star and been found. He would not let her be lost again, stifled in a world in which she could not defend herself. Morgan hadn't chosen to be a teacher lightly.

Or been chosen.

18

The flood of images, the caresses and shocks of the day were smoothed under the sea fog. Morgan's toes leaned together on the footstool like weary soldiers. The firelight consumed itself, died to a pure orange. His hands lost their awareness, then he went to sleep in the glow of the hesitating lamp.

The firelight smouldered gold from the core of the logs through the parched black bark.

Sibbi woke under her eyelids, just so far. She opened her eyes wide, open as an owl. Only preyed upon. The kindling, dry and sassy, spilled from Jason's hands into the fire, caught and raged, red, gold, blue, white until the walls crackled, cloth fluttered helplessly, a glass broke. The heat, the inferno in a night fog. The creatures woke up. Moths came on night-wet wings, mice fled into the paths of owl and fox. It set the fog on fire with light, the cold, chill grey swirled and sucked in the night. Inside there was nothing but the fierce shadow created to keep down the white heat. Outside, the soles of her feet scorched, heat shattered on her skin, the shape of flame ran over her like wind. Inside, the jaws of an animal trap made of ice and glass, bit and mangled her. The acid of fear raced through her veins, enraged her heart until it beat with fury inside its cage of ribs. Sweat poured out of her pores and froze.

As she slept, the moon danced on the surface of her body, setting small fires shaped like triangles on a rippling sea. She woke and slept in the voyages of her blood.

At dawn, Sibbi woke and looked out the window beside and above her bed. The geranium was dead, she saw, and in its place slender alders groped in the early light, rubbing their leaves in the first promise of warmth. She pushed back the quilt and sat on the edge of the cot. Her arms were sore and she rubbed them to get warm. She had a large soft white shirt on, much like her smock. The sleeves were rolled up to her wrists. She stuck her arms out in front of her to see them and flexed her hands like cat's paws, trailing her fingers in the air. She got up, went to the sink, took a towel down, dipped one end of it into the stale dishwater and washed her face. She did not feel the sting of the cold water. Then she hung the towel up on top of the others. The door made no sound when she went out to relieve herself in the dewy grass. She looked around in the light of red-tinged cloud and mist. She found the well. Opening the top she saw the bucket gently rocking in the deep pool, pulled it up half full and set it down on the edge of the well. By crouching slightly, she was able to tip it to her mouth. She drank until she was short of breath and her stomach was full. She was sick, rested and drank again until her stomach swelled hard and bloated. She stood at the edge of the well and watched the fish in the clear pool swimming round and round. She knocked all the bugs off the edge of the well into the water for the fish to eat. While she did all this and waited, the dryness left her fingers; she could feel her lips again; her skin smoothed out. Above her, the sky whitened and the wind came up from the sea. Sibbi turned and went back into the house, leaving the door ajar. Silently she went in and sat at the table. She broke off a piece of bread, swabbed it in the butter on the plate and ate hungrily. Her stomach grumbled. She finished one hunk and began another. When she finished she leaned her chin down on the table and blew the crumbs off onto the floor. She laid her cheek on the cool worn wood and listened to the plaid of sounds that came through the table. Sibbi fell asleep again while the room grew white in the morning.

Morgan woke uncomfortably stiff and cramped. He lifted his head out of the corner of the chair and opened his eyes, taking a moment to remember why he had slept in the kitchen. He rubbed the sleep out of his eyes and scratched his palms over the night's growth of beard on his chin. His eyes went to the cot. Gone! He started up, grabbing the blanket in his fist, his feet dropping to the floor. Sibbi sat up like a prairie dog, her arms dropped to her sides, her neck craning up. Morgan found her eyes riveted on him, icy blue pools.

"Sibbi, are you asleep?"

Dark shadows and the rustling of alders, the blood began to beat behind her eyes until she was blind. She tried to hold onto the chair, but her hands would not grasp it. Silver light coiled around her and a fire started in her brain. She must get down from this mountain before she was consumed. While her legs could still hold her body. While she could still feel the waves of air that seemed to carry a sound. . . .

"Sibbi, Sibbi. . . ." Morgan jumped up as she reeled out of the chair. He grabbed her before she hit the ground, but she had fled and her body went limp in his arms, white, yet she was soaking wet. He laid her back on the cot and put the quilt over her. With a dry cloth he wiped her face, which had relaxed, the fearful contortions of a moment ago gone. Morgan sat down on the edge of the cot, his hand upon hers.

When sure she was quiet, he got up to prepare for the day. While Sibbi lay in a heavy sleep, Mrs. Clery came with a bundle of clothes. Morgan stood with his hands stuffed into his pockets while she laid out each item.

"Had to guess at her size, thought she's probably near to my Sarah." There was underwear, a chemise, nightgown, petticoat with a new tie on it, a worn thin blouse of faded yellow and a blue serge jumper. "And a ribbon for when her hair comes out again."

"Thank you, ma'am, very much."

"Has she woken up, Mr. Morgan?"

"Yes, once I think, she seems to have washed and got a drink from the well and had some bread and butter. When I woke she was asleep at the table, but she sat up. I don't know what happened then, she fainted or something, got scared maybe, and didn't have the energy to fight it."

Mrs. Clery smoothed her apron, looked over her ample

shoulder to Sibbi. "I just don't know how you're going to manage without a woman; having them in school is one thing, but all day and all night is another, and her with more moods I'll warrant than most. . . ."

"I can't send her away, I just can't. I've seen those places she'd be taken to and I couldn't deliberately condemn anyone to that, not without trying." He was walking around the table. He placed his hands on the piles of clothes as if to keep them down, to keep her there, in place. "She's bothered," he looked up. "You're right, more moods than most. And not only moods, I'm afraid."

"What do you mean?"

"Oh, nothing dangerous, except perhaps to herself."

"Maybe if she went to the hospital there'd be people to help her and she could start over."

"I'll help her if anyone can. She's nowhere now, I really believe she doesn't know where she is or what she knows. She may not remember anything of what happened, it's impossible to tell."

"Well, you know I've tried to help but, Mr. Morgan, there's a lot of children down in my village, many I've helped deliver myself and we've got to protect them."

"She won't hurt anyone. All she needs is not to be hurt anymore herself, to have someone to hold onto her. She's not a stranger to me as she is to the village."

"Well of course, I know from the children that she's come to school, but they say she never says anything or does anything, just sits there like a lump."

"Children don't always like someone who's different."

"I didn't say they didn't like her, but of course they don't. It's difficult to like someone who's hardly there. As you said, no-one knows her."

"But I do—I think I do. She's worth something." And the hard sunlight streamed into the room. Mrs. Clery felt affronted and pursed up her lips. Morgan continued, "Have

22

you ever seen the seven-year-olds playing, 'I am happy, you are sad'? Two of them stand well apart, then run at each other with these faces on; they reach and grab each other, hugging and swinging round, both shouting, 'I am happy, I am happy' And the child who's watching begins to hug herself, wraps her arms round herself because no-one else is hugging her. You want to go and play with the left-out child, you want her to have someone to run at across the grass, someone with a happy face on, someone to grab the sad face, squeeze it out, throw it away. You want that child to feel the way the others do."

"Yes," she replied, her voice gone all soft and receiving. "And I'll keep an eye and ear out for more clothes for her." She gathered the paper and string, folded them and put them in her basket. "I'll be going then." She put on her scarf, for the wind was quite high at this end of the road. She tied a good knot under her chin. When she was part way down the path she turned and called, into the wind, "She's not all done growing yet, there's some seasons left." And she waved with her free arm.

Morgan felt he would no longer have to justify his devotion.

2

Indeed, when he finally saw the village, Morgan did think he had come to the ends of the earth. He had left the city, watching the green of grass and tree take over. On the train with the smells of so many journeyings in it, he couldn't be sure of anything, any direction, any end. The train wheels rattling on the rails under him and his suitcases: all he had to take with him. He opened the top of the window and let the smell of the countryside, greener still, come in and confuse him further. The towns came less frequently, became each one more distinct, more singular, for they spoke of people, where none seemed to exist between the stations. In the city he had never thought about all the people around him, as one grain of sand isn't aware of another on a beach, but out here with the desperation of seeking one's own kind, he saw all the faces, took a gesture or a look away with him to last to the next stop. And the more he became aware of the faces the less he could remember his own. This was loneliness. Nothing to identify him.

Under the steady hooves of the wheels, Morgan began a letter to his old teacher, but it was too shaky to write. "Dear Mr. Weaver: I am going to the ends of the earth, the end of the line, surely the tracks cannot run on forever like this. Around each curve, when you think it must stop, there is yet another stretch of track and beyond that another curve. . . ."

Morgan sank into the lumpy seat alone and tried to read. The light outside was failing. When it was altogether gone he couldn't read for the sight of his own reflection in the window that had turned into a mirror when the lights came on. He turned off the light above his seat and leaned his head into the corner between seat and wall. He pulled his collar close up to his neck and leaned back. He turned his eyes to the window, to the world that was reduced to flashing trees caught in the night in the passing light of the train. It was hypnotic. Fear drained away as he himself seemed to drain away out of the window, into the unexpected wholeness of the dark.

The next morning, feeling worse than ever, his suit rumpled, slept in, his face with a young beard and his hands dirty from his suitcases, Morgan arrived. The feel of the train had been shaken out of him by the bus ride from the last reach of the train tracks to the village. Samphire Cove, where they needed a teacher; there was no-one else. He was to be the only one to teach the children. The bus let him off, then made a huge circle and chugged off again. Morgan stood for a moment to regain his balance, to gather himself and to count his luggage. "Well, I'm somewhere I suppose," he thought. It was still very early and no-one seemed about.

Mist lay like wreaths around the houses, in the hollows between the houses, making the whole town look as if it were floating. Through the shimmering vapour he could see the road unravelling toward the crossing that must be the centre of things. The crossroad ran up a gentle hill on the one side, pocked with houses farther and farther apart, with barns and sheds behind them. On the other side the road took a quick dive into the harbour. Boats hung everywhere in the harbour. Boats with prows into the wind unless they were held between two moorings or bound with ropes as firm as fog to the pier. The road Morgan was standing on took a little swoop, then trailed up a fairly steep rocky bluff to a tight brown, stone-and-wood building visible in the wind, throwing a clear dark shadow onto the tall unkempt grass west of it. The sun was shining up there at least.

Morgan hoisted a suitcase under each arm and took the rest in his hands so he couldn't have chased away a fly from his cheek. If he had not been distracted by the effort of carrying all his bundles he might have panicked; there was absolutely nobody anywhere. Morgan panted past several quiet housefronts, yellow, grey, brown, white, green, blue, red and yellow again. Finally, with the mist still wrapped around his ankles and an overwhelming desire to throw his bags into the harbour, he reached the crossroads. Several three-storey buildings leaned over him, their doors mere inches from the truck ruts. No colour here but the hue of salt and weather. Morgan, usually mild, in his exhaustion was becoming angry. He had come miles and hours, he was tired and dishevelled and no-one appeared to greet him. He put the cases down on the slip of a wooden sidewalk outside the general store. Across the road there was a grocery with tumbled produce in the window on a slanting display board.

The double doors were shut. Diagonally opposite was a mail-order outlet with stoves and fridges standing like icebergs along the walls. On the last corner was a garage. The doors stood wide open, a dusty green pickup sticking its nose out. In front was a boat-haul with a new white rowboat upside down. Morgan started to cross the street toward the garage. Suddenly a red truck bounced into the crossroads, nearly knocking him down. It stopped and a burly man in a red plaid shirt leaned out from the high cab.

"Thank God!" Morgan said. Here was a human being.

"For nearly killing you?" said the man. "Who be you, mister?"

"I'm the new teacher." He was aware of how very new he must look, his wrinkled suit, his eyes squinting into the white sky. "Don't squint, Morgan, you look like a wee babe," he could hear his aunt say.

"Oh, the schoolmaster are you, we didn't know when to expect you."

"I'd be obliged if you would show me the way to the school. I understand my house is attached to it."

"Sure, it's up the end of the road there, on the hill."

It was the taut little wood-and-stone building he had seen standing in the long grass, clear on the bluff in the sunshine.

"I don't suppose you could give me a lift; I've got all these bags with me," indicating the heap on the dusty sidewalk.

"Sure, I'll just turn round." The idle motor roared in the dead quiet. Morgan gathered his belongings and threw them in the back of the truck with the fish nets and barrels. The man opened the cab door.

"Tom, and you then?"

"Morgan."

They roared up the road, straining the springs on the little-used drive. Morgan felt the sun and a warm gust of wind heavy with the smell of seaweed. The truck stopped and he retrieved his bags.

"The door's open."

"Thanks, thanks so much," his hand shielding his brow.

The man did not acknowledge his words. He turned the truck round again, paused, leaned out the window. "I've no kids myself, but I'll be seeing you." He drove away, rattling like heavy chains, disappearing like a red beetle into the ground.

The silence was stunning for a while, then Morgan began to hear the sea rolling on the rocks and the murmur of slipping grass. The panorama was magnificent, the huge carpet of sea, the rough grass-clothed hills rippling from the edge of the sea to the lid of dark trees, sensuously following the curves and hollows of the land. A small footpath led away, meandering toward the headland. He would explore later. He relaxed for the first time in weeks; time in this quiet seemed to yawn like seasons.

Curiously he turned to the house. It was irregular, a core of stone, with wooden parts added on. It seemed in good condition. He opened the heavy wooden door; it had no squeak. First there was a large pantry, then through another door the kitchen, but it seemed to be the living-room too. A stove, sink, small old fridge along one side. There was a curtain on a rod that could be pulled across to hide them. A table, a chair with a new cushion. An upholstered chair and needlework footstool in front of it. A fireplace and behind it he could see into another room through an open door. Bed, dresser, braided rug on the broad board floor, coat-rack and blanket-chest. New curtains hung still against the closed window. It was clean but stale. Morgan opened windows. The breeze rushed through and the rooms came alive with fluttering cloth. But it was not his yet.

Morgan brought in his suitcases and laid them here and there, on the bed and the table. He took out his radio and plugged it in to see if the outside world could still be heard.

Noises crackled in. He found a station and listened for a while as he unpacked, then the sound merely kept him company. He hung up his clothes, filled the drawers, propped up a picture of his family, in black and starch, on the dresser. There was one bookshelf along half a wall. He had a suitcase full of books and papers, which he carefully placed on the shelves. He found a nail in the yellowed plaster above the books and hung his diploma on it from a string. Mid-morning he ate the rest of his sandwiches, gone dry, then he found the well outside and hauled up a bucket of water.

"Well, hello there," he said in surprise to the heavy fish swimming slowly, lazily in a circle. "I'd better put you back." The next time the fish stayed under.

By evening Morgan was unpacked and the bags stowed away. He had been to town, to the grocery and got someone to bring up a load of food. He had met a few people and told them he was the new schoolmaster, as Tom had called him. At this moment it gave him ocurage to say that; he needed to feel master of something, though everyone was cordial. He fixed himself some sausages and bread and drank a large glass of milk. He found some pots, pans, plates and utensils in the pantry. When supper was over he finally opened the door to the school from the kitchen.

It was a large room, a peaked ceiling at least two storeys high with huge beams running across it. Tall thin windows set a foot or so into stone walls ran all along one side and the back. On the other wall, some dusty maps, a bookcase with a glass front. Inside a disorder of dog-eared texts, workbooks and a box of dusty chalk. At the front on a platform was a lectern; to one side a desk and chair. Behind, to the other side, a blackboard on an easel. Morgan walked up behind the lectern. Below him in the gloom of evening lay the rows of evenly spaced desks. The edges of the benches he could see were worn round, the floor rippled in waves where feet had scuffed. The desk tops with a thin layer of dust, specked with ink, gouged, initialed and carved. He suddenly felt quite sick in the pit of his stomach. Maybe the sausages had been too highly seasoned. Or the water, there was always an adjustment to new water. He fled, closing the door behind him, and without lighting a single lamp took off his clothes and climbed into bed. He fell asleep clutching the brass bars of the bedstead above his head.

Morgan awoke in the first dawn. It was bitterly quiet. He could taste quiet. For a few minutes or forever he slid deliciously in and out of sleep, not sure which world was real, which was unreal. When he finally got up he felt slightly enchanted, not at all sure that this was not the beginning of his seven years' dwelling beneath a fairy hill. He put on his dressing-gown and went out the back door. In the fenced yard he found a shed, an outhouse, a roofed structure with a cord or so of split wood in it. A clothesline ran diagonally from two high posts. The grass was end-of-summer short.

Below in the village, he could see the lights on in the windows. The fog brushed in and out the cones of diffused light. He wondered what was going on, then heard the muffled metallic motors of the boats in the harbour. Glimpses of green and orange, all distinct edges lost. As the foghorn began lowing into the dawn, the boats fell smoothly, spontaneously into a single file. There was no wind—the solid fog insinuated itself into every opening in the land. The chain of boats disappeared under the grey blanket. Of them nothing was left but the fading sound—lost. For Morgan it was unusual to be up so early, he imagined doing this every day for months of every year. Climbing out of a warm bed, putting on layers and layers of woollens, then cold stiff slickers and black hip boots. A film of mist coating one's face. The glistening boats with wet decks. The dreaming harbour and the foghorn calling like a loon from an invisible cliff. The water, opaque glass, still and yielding as far as the mouth of the harbour. Beyond, the open sea, intimate and vast. The elusive wave, the immense tide-witched swells and the fish swimming cold.

Just before dinnertime Morgan looked out again. The fog had lifted, become cloud and blown away. The houses stood bright like mushrooms. The women of the village, with their hands wrapped up in flowered aprons or holding their smallest child on one hip thrust out, stood at their back doors peering out at the harbour entrance. The boats were coming in, sunk below their waterlines. One man at the wheel, the other far astern, his eyes searching the water. The engines rattled full open, for the waves were coming in fast. The boats ran between the troughs, racing each other, wave and boat on collision with the harbour waiting. The moment they were inside, they cut the engines and coasted on the swell. The piers came alive with the deliberate methodical work of unloading the catch. The women turned to their homes, the children scattered. All the shadows were gone.

Morgan breathed again too. Like many men who work with their minds, he found this scene, which had just been acted out as it had been for generations, infinitely romantic, totally true and complete. A reason and meaning, basic, irrefutable, appealing. He felt these men had a knowledge he could never have, a knowledge akin to instinct, of bone and sinew. They were doing something he would never dare to do. He came to the sea as to a stranger, with no less awe than the fishermen. The sea awakened the poems in his blood, but he could never roll up his sleeves and pull a fish out of a trough in the sea. Morgan had a different relationship with the world, not better, not worse. He would try to give these children a vision out of his world, out of his experience, as they were to give him a vision out of theirs.

The next day, with heavy rain falling out of such a dark sky that everyone had their lights on all day, Morgan began the organization of his lessons. Able to work for a while amid the spread of notebooks, paper, pencils, he soon couldn't think creatively, found himself always returning to the window white with rain. In the afternoon he went into the schoolroom and housecleaned, breaking off last year's pieces of chewing-gum from under the desks, seeing what was in the bookcases and finding more dust inside than out. He repaired the maps on the wall with tape. And still the rain fell, so hard that the sound of the sea was lost. It made Morgan uneasy to lose that sound; he was growing accustomed to it. The rain had subdued even the sea. It felt strange to be moving around when everything was still, the animals all hidden; only the occasional gull was to be seen, briefly through the unfathomable sky. There was no wind, so the only movement in the trees was caused by the weight of the rain on the leaves. Morgan finally gave up. He turned his chair around and sat with his feet propped up on the windowsill watching the rain, listening to the rain and drifting into sleep.

He lapsed into a routine in which he felt comfortable. His comings and goings in the village were predictable, so the people felt at ease with him. He wrote his name on a piece of paper and opened an account with the bank. He bought a few things at the general store and established his credit. A little company of women came to the door one day with home baking and a quilt they said had not been finished before he came, otherwise it would have been on the bed for his arrival. He grinned and thanked them. He asked if they had children he would be teaching, and began learning who was who and who belonged to whom.

One afternoon while he was writing to Mr. Weaver, he heard the shuffling of bodies outside. Some of the children had come to peer at him.

The year swung on and one night in September Morgan set the bell alarum-clock that ticked unceasingly beside his bed. His clothes were all laid out pressed and clean. His shoes shined. In the schoolroom each desk was dusted and at his desk on the platform, a fresh pile of copybooks and a new box of pencils. The well-used texts were on the book-shelves in tidy rows. On the shelf under the lectern were Morgan's own books with a hundred book marks where he hoped to read to them.

The night was endless until he fell asleep, then instantly it was morning, the alarum ringing in his ear. The sun was fitful through the clouds. Too nervous to eat, he got dressed and built a fire in the stove. He washed his hands. He watched the clock. He walked around the classroom. Returned to the clock. Opened the school door. Stirred the fire again. The sun went behind a cloud, then came out again. Morgan consulted the clock once more and took it with him to his desk. He went outside to the corner of the stone build-ing where the bell hung and rang it, holding his ear, until he saw the children being disgorged from front doors and gathering in a scraggly line in the middle of the road. More and more came, kept coming, multiplying in the road. Morgan was seeing hundreds and hundreds of children of all shapes and sizes coming up the road, his road. He hung onto the bell-pull tightly, buttoned his coat so they would not be able to see his heart staggering around in his chest. He stood up straight, locking his knees. There was a lot of noise but he couldn't understand any of the words. He searched for faces that he knew. He thought by now he would have seen every child the village could offer, but many of these faces looked strange. The children jostled; the boys poked each other, the girls walked arm in arm. Some older children held a little sister or brother firmly by the wrist. Morgan stood outside and watched the procession, watched the little heads pass beneath the high door-frame. All varieties of black, brown and golden hair passed under his eyes.

When the last straggler had run in the door, Morgan took a deep breath and walked in himself.

"Shut up, Jimmy, and sit down, or I'll tell."

"Get off, Willy, you'll contaminate the whole bench."

"But that's where I sat last year."

"Don't care, anyway."

"Gimme that back, my mother'll kill me if. . ."

"Well, look who's here again." Aside: "Didn't she graduate last year?"

"Hey, this is the girl's side, get back to your own, you. . . ."

"Its alright Patty, stop crying, I'll be right back there, hold onto Mark's hand, here."

"I will not!"

"Sit here by me, sweetie."

"Shut up, will you?"

"You shut up."

The little girl up front sat properly in her seat and screamed; the little boy next to her stared solemnly over the back of his seat at the sea of chaos. A wiry boy with a shock of hair hiding his face climbed up over the desk to the row in front. Morgan reached out for him but intercepted a fist destined for a nose instead. The kid froze.

From another quarter, "I'll get you. . . ."

"Not if I get you first."

"That's my scarf."

"Well whatd'ya take it off for?"

Morgan shut the door with a bang. He listened. There did seem to be the beginnings of quiet. Pebbles of gossip. And when he turned to walk up to the front of the room, most of the eyes followed him.

"Ooooh, he's nice."

". . . hell I will."

Giggles. Then the only sound was the feeble sob of Patty below him. Her older sister got up and went to her. Took her by the arms and shook her, said awful words under her breath, and gave her an out-sized handkerchief.

"Sorry, sir, it's her first time." And she went back to her

seat. Morgan replied with a wave of his hand. He took hold of the lectern and said, "well" to himself and "hello" to the class.

Every eye was riveted on him. All stages of disbelief, he thought. He searched for a friendly face, found none, found a noncommittal face in the crowd and spoke to it.

"My name is Mr. Morgan, it's on the board there." He looked to it himself for reassurance. "And I should like you all to tell me yours. . . ."

The lunch hour gave Morgan no time to recover; it was only after they were all gone back down the road, their passage already imprinted in the flattened weeds, that Morgan came to himself. The scribblers were all still on his desk, the pencils too. The texts untouched in the bookcase. His head swirled with names, faces, the strident array of voices. Children thick and thin, tall and small, glib and dumb. Trying to learn just their names, he'd had to abandon trying to understand them. He had some supper with the seating chart he had spent most of the day making propped up on a vase in front of him. There were flowers in it, three of the girls had brought him a bouquet of nearly-dead fall flowers after lunch, giving it all together so as not to be open to scorn as individuals. The flowers drooped over Morgan's dinner. hiding the chart. He tried association, he tried sheer force of memory, all to no avail, he could only remember a third or so, and those the more overt ones. What had he managed on the first important day of school: to make a seating chart; to stop Patty from crying with the help of her sister; to return the scarf to its rightful owner; to get the little boy, overweight and coarse-featured, who would contaminate the bench, a seat somewhere. He'd heard all their names and ages, in fact every time they stood up he asked for names again as if they were prisoners of war. He hadn't got a single word out of the tiny Mark, who sat nearly the whole day with his eyes toward the rest of the class, his body

34

bent until Morgan thought he must have a terrible back-ache. He had excused more than half the class, all the boys and one very little girl, to go to the washroom. (He wondered who was supposed to supply the toilet paper.) His final act of the day had been to bandage a bruised hand that had had a desk top dropped on it—accidentally.

3

Morgan and Sibbi lived physically parallel lives. Wagon ruts in the same road with the grass of centuries between. She showed no inclination to leave. She lived in the highlands of her own mind and walked on the same floors as Morgan.

He sat at his desk to work on lessons or to write, his pipe resting in the ashtray in danger of being buried by papers. He sat in the comfortable chair to read. He did chores around the small rooms and ate by himself. His eyes strayed now and again to Sibbi. She did everything for herself. She got up sometimes to wash, very carefully. She helped herself to food—bread, cheese, cold meat, whole raw carrots—and got a clean glass from the shelf to pour herself a glass of milk. She rinsed and dried the glass and returned it to the shelf. She visited the fish in the well every day. She sat on the floor or in the grass in the sun and rocked back and forth over her crossed legs. She never looked at Morgan. She never looked at herself in the mirror. She had not yet touched her own head. If she watched anything, it was the wind in the grass or the fish. She avoided flame: the fire and the lamps. One day she was outside while Morgan was chopping up kindling and he looked just in time to see her staring up at the sun. He went and stood over her until his shadow came across her eyes, for she would have blinded herself. Sometimes she pressed herself against the wall or the floor until every small curve of her body was flattened. When she was uncomfortable with her clothes on she took them off and put on the nightgown.

She sat on the edge of the cot, mid-day awake, her knees apart, her hands holding onto a knot of blanket. Vacant stare, but her eyelids were uneasy, quivering, the lashes beating like wings. She breathed through dry half-parted lips. Morgan got up from his chair at the desk, gently, quietly. He went over to her, crouched on his heels and put his hands carefully on her shoulder bones. Her eyes dropped to avoid his gaze and wavered back and forth as if she were on a swing. Then very slowly, with a blind groping motion, her hands came up, hovering in the space between them; her hands thinking, separate from the rest of her. Her breath followed, became more shallow. Then her fingers stretched out; she touched his hands on her shoulders. The fingers curled slightly, relaxed and still they touched him. She discovered his knuckles, examined each one separately, brushed the hair on the back of his fingers, reached tentatively to his nails, then back to his wrists, over the bones. She began to move up his arm, then softly as the fluff leaving a dandelion, her fingers lifted, curled into loose fists that came together at her breast. Her breath coming in an audible gasp was the only sign of her ordeal. She opened her hands, palms up, holding them close together as if to see them both with one eye. Morgan wondered what she saw there. No sign. They were clean and small, but marked with callouses and wiry muscles in her fingers. She put them down and lifted her face, her eyes, right into Morgan's. He felt the tremor that ran through her like quicksilver; but in her eyes, was that recognition? Fear? What was it her eyes were saying? He wanted to shake her and was surprised he did not.

She slept, keeping the hours of a wolf.

When Morgan broke the silence, began talking to her, and to himself again, there was no change. He talked all the time she was awake; he talked about everything he did, talked to the bed, the fire, the bread knife and carrots, the water pail and the wind. He told her when the sun was shining. He told her when it rained and the ground was swollen like a sponge. "Come and feel the ground Sibbi," he took her hand from its nowhere place in her lap, but there was no response. "Another day perhaps. One thing we know is that it will rain again, don't we?" But there was no *we*. Morgan talked all the time for a week until he was tired of the sound of his own voice. He wore grooves in himself, but made not the slightest impression on Sibbi. Only when he leaned over her in her sleep and whispered her name did he get a response, a sharp intake of breath from the sub-terranean caves of memory. He did it often to preserve his own sanity. When she scraped her legs on a rock, the cut bled itself clean before Morgan saw it, for she had made no sound. When she went out to the well in a deluge and got soaking wet, it was Morgan who changed her clothes and put a blanket on her shivering body while her eyes dreamed apart.

He grew tense and irritable and frequently walked down to the village, where he smiled and said hello to everyone just to be recognized, to get an answer, even if some of the people did look at him peculiarly. He did a little shopping to have a brown bag in his hand. He stood on the sidewalk outside the store to have a chat with anyone who passed by. He stopped in at the garage and talked and listened and watched real live human beings. He walked around on the pier talking to the fishermen, who were repairing their boats. He asked the children how they were enjoying their summer holidays. He helped Mrs. Stanney, the postman's wife, carry her groceries home and, yes, he stopped in to have a cup of tea, much to her surprise and irritation, for she had wanted to get the groceries put away before supper. Morgan avoided talking about Sibbi though everyone was curious. "Oh, she's doing fine, as well as can be expected," and asked a question of his own.

When he finally had to go home; when it would be too dark to find his way after the fog rolled in, he'd find her pale, quiet, pinned to the board of her own silence.

"Damn it Sibbi, go outside and let me eat in peace." She was motionless. He got up and grabbed her arm, pulled her over to the table, dragged a stool across on two of its legs and set it opposite his chair. He put the stool behind her, took her shoulders and sat her down hard. Involuntarily she held the edge of the table with both hands to keep from falling. He put a plate in front of her, put a piece of bread and fruit on it. He went back to his chair and sat down again. "Now, at least, it *looks* as if I have company." He took a spoonful of soup, watching that for a moment. When he looked up again, defiantly, daring her to move, he met her eyes, ice blue in a face drained of colour. This time was different. He put his spoon down silently, his eyes not leaving hers. She was actually looking at him.

"Sibbi." Whispered. "Sibbi, what do you see? Do you see me? Sibbi? Try. . . try. . . ." And her brow wrinkled, her mouth closed, her lips curled inward, she slipped her teeth over her lower lip and let it slide out again. "Sibbi, please try longer, harder, hold onto whatever it is. . . try. . . ." He lost her eyes, they withdrew, went down, but she *was* looking, seeing where she was.

Sibbi saw her own hands on the table first, then her glance went to the floor; across to the corner where it met the wall she saw that the floor was dark, and the wall light above it. There were dark shapes on the wall, but she wasn't sure what they were. In the far corner a soft rounded shape and above it another darkness, tall and shiny. Her eyes ran up to the top of the window. It was a great height. The darkness was two things at once, something unseen but real, and something reflected, unreal, dangerous. Shadows and images,

38

formed in darkness, amorphous, meaningless, moving. . . .

"Sibbi," called Morgan, loudly for he could see she was caught. "Sibbi. . . ." Her body tightening, coiling. "Sibbi. . . ."

Smoke, on the shiny surface, silver and black. Faint as fog on the smooth surface of the sea, she heard or saw the sound. One moment noise, loud, shattering the blood in her ears; a moment before or after, dust on the dry bones in her ears. She bent her head between her hands. Streaking, chasing pains in her head.

Her body curled up like a piece of burnt paper.

Morgan reached across the table, put his hands on her head, pressed it hard between them, rubbed down the back of her neck, trying to undo the knotted cords.

His hands covered her ears for her and when he took them back up to the top of her head the roaring was gone. She felt the weight of something on her head, something moving, encompassing, gathering, something making the pain hide.

Morgan felt her trying to lift her head. He helped her, moving his palms around to the sides of her face.

The new shadows stabbed once at her through her open eyes, then were gone, banished.

She was drenched and panting and colour flushed in her cheeks. Her eyes were misty. Morgan dropped one hand on hers, lying limp on the table.

"Come here, Sibbi, come around the table, come to me. Come here. . . ." Slowly, sonorously, sung into her night, thinking she could maybe hear this time, maybe understand. "Come here. . . come here. . . ." And she got up weakly, trembling from exhaustion, but she wasn't only being called this time, he was sure she was coming, aware. She was coming like the tiny child who had been found, out of the darkest night. Around the table, around the whole world, around several worlds. Morgan slid his hands up her cold wet arms.

39

Sibbi felt the weight on her skin, she saw a pale warm light like wheat.

She was leaning and not falling.

Morgan pulled her onto his lap and gently put his arms around her cold body. Only her face was hot, burning his skin when he pressed her head to his neck, covered her cheek and closed her eyes with his fingers.

The shadow was tame beneath her eyelids, all of one colour, uncommitted, at peace.

He held onto her like one rescued from the sea. She had come to him, once.

The next time he saw her, she was warm and dry and apart. Pliable, her eyes as opaque as fish scales. She reached up as far as her ears, ran her fingertips around the hollows and folds. Her eyes looked as if they were trying to turn inward.

"Yes, Sibbi," said Morgan with fatigue in his voice, the tone that crept in when he was dealing with a very dull child. "Yes, those are your ears, you are hearing my voice with your ears." But she wasn't, she was listening to the sound of her skin on her skin, finding more of her body. Then she had hands and ears and one private sound. She covered her ears with her flat palms and listened. Morgan thought she was shutting out his voice. She listened and the roar began. Her hands darted away, poised open. The thundering subsided. She put her hands in her lap and began to rock back and forth. She was sitting on the floor in front of her cot. Her head was slightly thrown back, small, delicate, the tufts of hair swaying like tassels of corn silk. She was as good as asleep behind her eyes, her lids bobbing in the rhythm of her rocking, but she didn't close them all the way as if afraid of what she might find behind them.

The sun lay in stripes on the floor, coming in the open door and windows. It was warm on Morgan's shoulders. He went back to his lessons. New books had arrived and he was working to adapt them to his classes. Autumn was coming. School would begin again soon. The air was thick and lazy, heavy with the mature ripe season. The days were saturated with pollen and fruit. Trees were deep green, the forest with bottomless blue shadowed depths. Birds and animals were quieter now, like the fields, turning gold and the sedge grass on the bluff turning brown. Even the pull of the tide-waters on the beach seemed gentler. The land was hot and tired, its surface scored and dried by the wind.

It took Morgan longer to do the same old things, and he gave a thought now and again to winter, but he had no time to look under the rock that buried Sibbi. He wasn't even irritated that she seemed to have forgotten the time he had held her against the night. He talked to her now when he felt like it, worried less at her silence, troubled about her less.

There were several beginnings in a year: the arbitrary calendar, which began close to the shortest day; spring in its prosaic rush of furious weathers and poetic nuances of green life, of breaking ground; and now, in the waiting for the crisp clear days of fall, the energy of red, the philosophy of gold, the beginning of a new school year. The new growth in the children seen after their absence, their bodies bigger in the same small desks. New scribblers and pencils, sleek and smooth, untouched. The anticipation of a blank piece of paper, the promise. Morgan's season of hope.

Sibbi saw her own hands now and touched her ears. She did not go near Morgan. Then in the evening when he opened the door to the schoolroom and went in to give it the last touches, make the last arrangements, she came to the door.

A huge dim cave exploded out of a stone. Pure silver was caught, framed in headstones on the walls of the cave. Yet the shape was familiar; why was the moon here when the walls were sand? The moonlight caught on a white shirt and a disembodied figure swam in the dark.

"What is it, Sibbi?" Morgan saw her silhouette in the rectangle of the doorframe. "I'm just getting ready for tomorrow." He looked at her. She looked at the talking shirt. "The children come tomorrow, Sibbi, back to school." He couldn't see her face. Her arms hung like ropes at her sides. He was excited by the prospect of school and felt her an intruder in this private moment, his last chance to be alone in the room. "It'll be nice to have them all back," speaking to himself.

Then in her oblique remembering, Sibbi lifted her hand to her brow, as she had so often in this room, lifted her hand to push her hair back off her face. Her hand found nothing there. The other hand came up—quickly. She felt her head. Fingers to her face, eyes, nose, mouth, back over her ears to her hair. Down to the nape of her neck where her skin was cool in the open air. She grabbed a handful of hair and drew her hand out; nothing was left in her fingers. She did it again as if to calculate the distance.

Morgan wrenched out of himself, came to her, bumping desks, fearing for her, this discovery.

Horrible seams broke open in her head. In the chamber of the room an animal sound echoed. A black sound from a break in the moon. The silver of a knife-blade turning to gold in the furnace of flames. The man with fiery gold skin grabbing her hair and her screams. Hair thrown like hay onto the fire to burn and the pieces that fell in her face, grass strewn over an open grave. Flame swooned over her skin and she fought the walls, helplessly because she was tied, pounding her head on the door, rolling it back and forth, grinding it on the wood.

Morgan grabbed her, pinned her arms to her sides, kept his head above her thrashing. He dragged her to her bed, pushed her down, held her arms across her chest, knelt one leg across her thighs. She was amazingly strong. Her face was purple with rage, bloated, her lips bitten until they bled, her eyes lost in the contortions of flesh.

When she was finally still, Morgan saw that there were tears on her cheeks. Her breath still came in gasps and her nose was running. He released her, took the edge of a sheet and wiped her face dry. He lifted her arm and it fell back as if dead. When she opened her eyes sleepily, they were washed clear. She looked at Morgan as if pleading with him. Her stare wandered away, then returned.

"It's okay, Sibbi, it's just your hair; it'll grow back, it's already grown a bit, you're fine as you are. . . you're a pretty girl." That must be the right thing to say, even to her. She tried to find the edge of the sheet. When she did, she pulled it weakly over her face and hid from herself. She fell asleep very quickly and when it was deep enough, her breathing slow and steady, he covered her up for the night.

For the next few days she remained in hiding, under the covers. She came out only when Morgan was gone. From time to time she was aware of his presence, aware of herself. She slept many hours of the day and got up at night. Her memory simmered. She took a cloth handkerchief and tied it on her head. She plucked at her hair under the edges of the scarf, but often with a puzzled look on her face, not quite sure what it was.

Morgan slept fitfully that night before school and was weary the next day. The children stared curiously at him, at the door to his living rooms and then into his yard. There was nothing to see.

"Is Sibbi coming to school this year?" asked a very small girl, curious about she knew not what.

"Shut up," from the child next to her.

"Hush," and all eyes came up to Morgan.

"Well, I don't imagine for awhile, for a long while perhaps. . . . She is very sick Lynnie, it's like having a terrible headache. You've had a headache?"

She nodded solemnly.

43

"Like that, and she doesn't remember. If I brought her in here, she wouldn't remember any of you."

The children lost their sly curiosity and became more open.

"Is it true," another girl, stretching her lips, struggling, "Is it true about her brother, I mean, that he cut off all her hair?"

"Yes, it is." The memory was his too.

"And he left her all alone," from a littler one.

"And he beat her up, real bad."

"Who told you that?" The girl shut her lips tight. "No, I'm not prying."

"It's just the talk around, sir, everybody's curious," from an older boy. "You were curious yourself about her, right from the beginning," boldly.

"Yes, that's true, I said I wasn't prying. I just don't want her to turn into gossip."

But that's all she could be, secluded as she was, the victim of a strange series of incidents.

"But is it true, about her being beat up?"

"Yes, it seems to be."

"And then he ran away?"

"Yes."

"Does she ever come out?"

"Yes, she goes into the yard sometimes, no farther though."

"Is she 'fraid she'll get lost?" From Lynnie. It seems incomprehensible that such a big girl could get lost.

"Probably not lost the way you mean, but that's actually what she is, Lynnie, she's lost, because she's forgotten. It's as if you were suddenly in a new house with new people all round you, only they all seemed to know you, but you couldn't remember any of them."

"Like my auntie when she comes for a visit."

"That's right."

44

"But, sir, can't anybody get her brother, or do something? I mean is it legal?"

"Well, he's probably far away by now. It wouldn't be good for her to see him again, I don't think."

"Oh, yeah."

"I'd like you children to do something for me. If you see her when you're coming or going, if she's outside, I wish you wouldn't ask her questions. Just say hello or whatever, but no questions." Their faces accepted this.

"The way she is now, how long'll she stay like that?"

"I don't know. . . . And now can we get to our work?"

The children dragged out their papers and opened their books for the first week of school.

Sibbi went outside, walked around and around the well in the dust, trailing her fingers along the edge while the fish swam round and round in the water. She remembered Morgan, now, even when he wasn't in sight. And wondered where he was, why there was a change in his habits. When she woke up in the morning he was gone. There were voices coming from behind the closed door. She went to the door and pressed herself against it. Her skin picked up the sound. She put her forehead, not her ear to the wood, for the vibration was too loud, and hurt her. Then she would drift away, feeling her way into the light, which she knew was warm. She went outside and lay in the thick drain-watered grass under the eyes of the pantry wall.

When she woke it was mid-afternoon and there was a great noise coming from somewhere. She found the ground and the sky; she got up and wandered to the edge of the house. She couldn't see very far and there was a great deal of shadow. A large blurred wave-like mass, noisy and shot with colour, was moving down the hill, going away. She blinked and made a grunting sound, trying to make it something. She moved out, held onto the rail fence and began rocking against it, still making the small animal sounds.

45

Whatever it was, it was now far away. The dust settled back onto the road. Sibbi sank back into her night while the long stretch of sunlight cast her shadow in front of her longer and longer until it disappeared over the bluff, where she couldn't follow. She put her arms out over the top rail, reaching toward the lost end of her shadow.

By dawn Saturday morning, the rain was coming down steadily. Sibbi got up and went to the window above the sink. A great cloud lay on the trees, turning them silver. The grass in the yard was beaten flat on the ground. After gathering on the roof, huge drops of rain fell off the edge, past the window. She chewed a raw starchy potato and watched the grey rain-water.

Morgan lay in bed until mid-morning, listening to the rain, luxuriating in his dry bed and the peace of Saturday. He could stay in all day, reading and dozing. He finally got up, made a huge breakfast of sausages, egg and fried potatoes, moving around Sibbi to prepare it. She stood transfixed at the sink like a post. He built just enough fire to keep the damp down and sat down with his pipe, his back to the stove. He felt quite alone and contented. The mercury in Sibbi seemed low today, her limbs somehow blurred and softened by the rain; the curve of her backbone was relaxed, neither limp nor taut. She was grey and weathered.

Morgan took up his book and read.

Into the grey waste that was Sibbi came patches of colour. She touched the dark brown pieces of wood that held the window glass; the limp curtains were yellow; she put her hand on the gunmetal-grey pump nozzle; it was heavy and cold. A piece of greasy red-checked oilcloth was on the work-table. She moved along the wall, sliding her palms over every inch she could reach, feeling the unevenness of the yellowing plaster. The knob on the door was burnished gold and green. She twisted it several times and felt the lock click in and out. Her cot was covered with white sheets and

46

a green blanket; she rubbed the blanket into all kinds of wrinkles. The table was brown with deep white scratches, the stool was beige, the chair brown and the cushion on it solid green. The fireplace was rough grey stone. She sat in front of the bookcase and traced her finger in the dust on the shelves, then crawled over and followed the green and brown and gold pattern on the back of the chair Morgan was sitting in. She traced the design on the rough material delicately as if painting the stylized flowers with her fingertip. She squeezed the cord that ran all round the edges of the chair. When she pressed flat on the back, the taut material sank in under her hand. She pushed herself and rolled onto her back beside the chair, her knees up, held tight against each other. Morgan looked down at her, then returned to his book. Her fingers were tingling from all their discoveries. She looked closely at them, the nails, the dirt. She bit on the nails. She sucked on her fingers and her gaze wandered up to the ceiling. It was high and light, the colour of a haystack, not at all like. . . like. . . but she could not remember what it was not at all like. Something about lying on her back, with her legs up, on the hard floor bothered her. She stretched to drive out whatever it was. The numbness in the centre of her bones, the forlorn pain that was buried there. She made fists, tightened the muscles in her arms until they quivered, then squeezed her arms against her stomach, drew her legs up over them until she was all rolled up in a ball.

Then for the first time she looked outside herself for something concrete to hold the tottering equilibrium inside. One hand reached out, up onto the arm of the chair, her fingers spread like the spokes in a spider web, seeking. She slid her open hand along the top until she came to Morgan's arm, his elbow bent out over the floor. She touched it, gently, tentatively feeling the heat coming into her cold fingers. Morgan watched the motion, the spidery crawl of the fingers

47

over his arm, the cold print of her skin. Then she held on with the strength of a trap and, in relief at having reached something, she put her cheek to her knee. She rocked from the bough of his arm.

"Are you having a rough time, Sibbi?" There was no answer but she didn't take her hand away. He made no move to hold her, to intervene in her struggle. Indeed the enemy was unknown. It was peculiar for him to have more information, more knowledge than she did at this moment. She was discovering the ground like a hunting hound, the territory unknown, but the instinct in the blood. Her past was a heritage, an inheritance. He wished he knew where she was in the labyrinth, in the serpentine trail she must follow to come out. He could only watch these refracted signals. Spying on an elusive fish pushing in and out of the swaying seaweed.

She heard a voice in the dark, but it was not nearly so close as flesh. Her own, when it was cold and damp with fear, repelled her, but this flesh she held of the man who came and went, willy-nilly, in and out of her circle, this was warm and quiet.

She began to drift out of her own circle into a soft senseless never-world. A dry leaf, her hand lifted and blew away. She sat up. She stood up weightless. The air supported her. She floated as easily as a wisp of fog into the grey rain.

4

When Sibbi was born under a bush, her mother died in the effort. She never imagined such a thing would happen. She had given birth easily and quickly to a first child, a boy, eleven years before and under the best of circumstances. So now, when things weren't so good and she had no money and no way to get to a hospital, she stayed at home. She was

48

not popular, her son wasn't liked on account of his wild ways and she had no husband. Her house had disintegrated until only the sheer strength of the oak corner-posts held together the abandoned shed that she called home. It hid in the trees, and that helped keep rain off the roof, but the trees shook their bugs into the shed and in wind storms beat with their branches against the shingles. In storms she and her son Jason sat together on the iron bed, blankets over their backs, clutching each other, watching the orange heat in the barrel stove and listening to the wind in the pipe chimney. Jason was very close to his mother. The side of him that went outside was tough, unyielding, defiant; the side of him that warmed to his mother was child-afraid, child-fragile. With her he could give up. When she went to town with her seasonal offerings of wild blackberries, hand-picked herbs, woven straw mats or rugs braided from bags of scraps she collected like a ragman in a wagon with built-up sides, Jason went with her, his stringy body lean and hard as an animal's. On the way back he pulled the wagon with its load of flour, oil, salt and sugar. His stomach already rumbling, his eyes bright and happy. They laughed and talked and admired the evening sky.

When a man came in the evenings, she sent Jason outside in the field to sleep under the old apple trees. He was not afraid. He lived a thousand shipwrecks under the spars of the boughs and the starry black sky, on a blanket in the middle of a swaying sea-field. It was alright with Jason that his mother had a man, it made her happy and warm. She sang him songs and listened to his heartbeats. She held his head and her love overflowed from her face to his.

"Oh, my lovely, special boy."

Then the man moved on and Jason was back in the shed, just in time, for by now the nights were frosty. And his mother got fatter, took off her sashes and belts and hung them up. She was different now. She didn't chase him, he had to come to her to be caught. When she held him the only hard part of her was her stomach, all the rest was soft.

She just took it into her head to have this "love-child," as she told Jason, out in the open clean air. It was spring and the shed was still winter-damp and cold. The trees wove a net above her in the sky. She crouched and pushed and pushed until the blue baby was born and the blood. She washed the baby with oil until it was pink and cried its lungs clean. But she was so tired and the blood didn't stop flowing down her legs. She had to crawl back to the shed, dragging the baby on a blanket. She was able to climb into bed and to open her breast to the hungry baby, propped against a pillow.

When dawn came and changed the sky to gold, when Jason woke up, he found that his mother was dead and the new baby was sucking hard.

A cold white woman picked the name Sybil out of a ledger and put a little bracelet on the baby girl's wrist. Jason sat in offices and waiting-rooms, in halls and wash-rooms. He listened to people whom he'd never seen before talk at him. Mostly he looked out of the windows and watched the translucent green come out on the spring-softened, oily-branched trees. They took away the wagon that he'd brought the baby in. He had to go back to the shed without it, in a truck with strangers who wrapped up his mother's body in her own bloody sheets and put it in the back of the truck.

"We'll take care of it, son." So he never saw her again.

Jason was shown to prospective foster-parents, but none wanted him. Finally, with a small satchel of his belongings in her hand, a woman took him to the orphanage. They emptied the contents on a huge desk. One pair of cord trousers, one wool plaid shirt, one scarf, one knitted stocking-cap, two pairs of mittens, one heavy jacket, one slicker, cracked and peeling to its rubber veneer, socks, underpants, shirt; his boots were on his feet already. Then they took the drawstring bag Jason had carried himself and emptied it on the desk. Two books with library stamps inside, slingshot, marbles, string, stone, nail, a worn-out clock, a pottery cup, a tiny blue china flower in a white china bowl, a paisley shawl with a deep golden fringe. His mother had been very careless with her things and this was all that was left. They told him to leave everything there on the desk and led him away. He never saw any of those things again.

Finally a man and his wife came to the orphanage looking for a boy to help them on their sheep farm. The man picked Jason out for his clever sharp eyes and sturdy body—the way he picked his dogs. Jason told the woman his eyes pleading, that he had a baby sister and could they see their way clear to take her too? She was small and beautiful and later she could help the woman around the house. So they agreed. The nursery gave up the solemn pale blue-eyed baby who nestled immediately in the woman's arms, endearing herself to her.

"Ah, she's so sweet, don't you think?"

Her husband grunted, unaccustomed as he was to babies.

Jason clung to her as long as she was small and held a memory of his past. But the little girl had no such memory and when she started growing into a person she began to chafe him. It was a strange thing to watch the way he circled around her, pulling away yet tied because she was the only tie. He wasn't complete without her, without his idea or illusion of her. In actual fact she was a separate solid human being, skin browned by the sun where it was exposed, hair bleached to a halo. Jason wanted her winter-white skin, pale, elusive, able to evoke spirits. He shook her off if she came to him, grabbing his knees and shouting with delight, her chin boring into his thigh, for then he wasn't ready. But she wouldn't always let him when he wanted to hold her; she squirmed and arched her back until she nearly fell out of

51

his arms. He was envious because she belonged totally to this place, these people. He didn't want to belong to strangers; he didn't want Sibbi to belong either.

When he was sixteen and a man and Sibbi was five, he felt ready. The secret he'd held inside until it fermented could come out. He would escape. Only the energy of his youth had sustained him so long, only the steel core that grew stronger each month had enabled him to save money and hide away supplies for the right moment.

He took Sibbi by her little chubby hand and led her into the barn. The whole inside was yellow with hay and straw and sun-dust. He sat her down on the end of a bench. She held onto it because everything seemed so grave. She crossed her ankles and swung them unconcernedly back and forth and craned her neck back to stare into the cathedral-gold depths of the ceiling. Jason caught her eyes.

"Look at me, Sibbi, I've got something to tell you and you must promise on death not to whisper a word to anyone."

Sibbi writhed uneasily, half anxious to know whatever it was, half unsure if she was willing to promise. She'd seen lambs die and be cut up for the stew-pot or, if they were too little like she was, thrown away over the cliff. She didn't fancy herself limp and cold like that.

"What if I don't want to know?"

"But you've got to because you're part of it."

"Part of what?"

"Promise."

"Okay, I promise not to tell."

"Not even her."

"Okay." She was used to him referring to her mother as *her*.

"We're going to get away from here."

"What a silly idea." Loudly into the air, just the way she'd heard Jason say those same words.

"It's not silly, it's true, and we're going to do it, everything is all planned and you're coming with me. I can take care of you now, I know enough to be apart."

Sibbi didn't want to be apart, she was just fine here, with a mother and father and fields and sheep and...

"She's not your mother, I've told you that before."

"But she loves me and takes care of me."

"I love you and I can take care of you now, don't you understand? These people are being paid to take care of you, like getting pocket money."

Sibbi put her head down. When she got pocket money it was for doing a chore, for doing something she really didn't want to do.

"We're going to go exploring, Sibbi, we're going to see what's over the next hill. Wouldn't you like that?"

"You're not as good to me as Ma... as she is."

"But I will be, Sibbi, when I'm taking care of you all by myself. I'll let you do all sorts of things; we'll have all sorts of adventures."

And because she had always been secure this seemed alright. Besides, she was a bit more afraid of disobeying Jason than her parents. Jason flew around like a tight little red hawk and the claws in his eyes were not always folded beneath his feathers. So Sibbi kept her word even though she moped around and was finally put to bed for a couple of days. And Jason, those last few days, was a changed boy, smiling, making small talk, doing things he wasn't asked to do, and stealing the last few things he thought they would need.

He had it all planned; they left together one bright morning with the two-wheeled cart full of eggs. Even Sibbi didn't know until he made a wide swing under the protection of a hill and they were going in the opposite direction from the town.

"This is it Sibbi, we're off!"

"But I didn't even say goodbye."

"Yes you did. I heard you."

"But not the right kind of goodbye."

"It's alright. Pretty soon you won't even remember. . . ," and he held her hand tighter, to pull her out of her pout. "Stop it, Sibbi; we've got a long way to go and you can't dawdle."

At his hiding place, he picked up the money and the clothes, the blankets and tarp, rope and knife. He put everything on top of the eggs and covered it all with the cloth. Some of the eggs broke and left a yolk trail behind them.

When they got to an outpost grocery Jason hid the cart, unloaded it, put all the good eggs in containers and took them in to sell at the store. The man said he hadn't seen him before. No, he was new around here, admitted Jason, and quickly stared him out of more questions. He took the money and went back to repack the cart. He was behind schedule. With Sibbi on top of the cart he walked more quickly. Jason had not been idle all those years, he'd studied maps until he knew just where he was going and how to hide. He knew where the dividing line between the communities was, knew if he could get across that line it wouldn't have to be in secret, for no-one would tell or even be interested except to know that they'd passed through. At times only his hawk-like fever kept him going and the knowledge of what would happen if he got caught.

That summer was a good one for travelling. There was fog to hide under when they needed it. The days were warm, with just enough breeze along the shore, so they made good time. The nights were quiet so they weren't too cold. Jason took Sibbi close to him to keep her warm. They huddled under the blanket as he and his mother had done long before. He talked to her constantly in the evenings and early mornings. On the road he was preoccupied with the distance and at night he slept hard. But these talkings were tilted, tinged with the fog of dawn or the pearly light of dusk.

Sibbi was glad for the company of a human voice, but she didn't know what he was talking about. He would tell her a story that flew over her head like a flock of migrating birds, the sky darkened by their wings, the air overwhelmed with cries. Then they were gone, the sky empty, hollow of sound. The only record of their passage was an echo in her inner ear.

Sibbi was not afraid, she was sometimes lonely and sad. She saw no cause for his moods; his kindnesses toward her weren't prompted by love or guilt, by her actions or his being, but were based on his own mental processes. She didn't assert herself; as a result she lost her place in Jason's scheme, as the one who needs to be noticed but is silent, never is. Jason filled up his hours without her. If she had something to say and waited timidly, politely, she waited forever until she forgot herself because he had figured her out of his time.

They fell into the routine of travel; their going took some sort of order. This left Sibbi with long hours to trudge alongside the cart, one browned hand holding onto the rail. First she relived her dreams until they dried up in the morning. Then she made up stories about where they were going, nebulous dreams with no other people in them, no distinct place, under a grass-spread cobweb somewhere. Before she got too hungry, she thought about her mother and father, Jason's *them*, said in an ugly voice. So she thought about them privately, only because it was just before supper the memories ended up being mostly about food, about apple pies, cakes, scones, butter tarts, soft gingerbread men, early sweet corn and lamb stew. On the road they ate porridge, stolen eggs and potatoes, raw vegetables and hard new apples. Sibbi wanted a glass of milk. Afterward she plodded along as empty in the head as Jason, the cart jerking her arm, sheer doggedness the only thing that kept her together. When Jason saw her nodding, he lifted her up onto the cart, set the old ragged umbrella he had found in a rubbish heap above her, wedged its handle in a corner of the cart and let her sleep in its shade, while through the holes the sun moved across her face, marking the passage of time.

In time the heath bloomed over the rock ledges. Golden-rod waved its plumes of pollen. Eye-bright was rampant in the August-dry meadows. Blackberries grew on the low hungry rocks. In time Jason ceased to be hunted, became the hunter. He was bronzed and toughened by the summer sun. In the necessity of the road, in the impulse of the hills, Jason began to trust himself. He had walked through many parts of himself, had overcome many doubts. He hid Sibbi in the low warm hollows and worked a day here and there for farmers in their fields, getting a meal and a few pennies. "Do a day's work, sir, for a supper and a small wage?" When he worked like a man, the men talked to him like a man or shared that strong man-silence. The women were sometimes for ruffling his unruly black hair, sometimes for serving him with the diffidence they would show to a grown man. Jason ate at their tables because he was so handsome, but he always refused to stay the night.

Sibbi was left in the most private sun-freckled hollow. Trees nodded all around, stretched long branches into the open light. The lean black-shadow limbs of trees lacing through the shuddering leaves. She perched on the cart, high, out of the way of snakes and bugs. When Jason left her, the trees were shrouded, soft, blue-grass; the birds were singing languorous clear songs with none of the frantic righteous passion of spring, feasting on the abundant summer crop of bugs in tree-bark, long grass and hidden dew-soft ground. In the half-light of morning lay the silvered cob-webs on the points and bent joints of grass. Sibbi thought they were abandoned or made by invisible spiders for there were never any to be seen. The webs shrivelled and blew away later on in the morning.

Sibbi lay on her back in her private silence and listened. She heard what her dead mother heard from under the ground; that lifetime when there is absolutely no wind. She heard a stone turn to sand. The sky did nothing while the sun loved her until she was warm.

And impatient. She watched a mosquito drink her blood until its belly was bloated and red, then she killed it. She watched an inch worm make an upside-down U a million times on a mile of stick. A cobweb still lay in the damp mossy roots of a tree. A huge grey jay sunbathed in the clearing. When she was hungry she ate blackberries until her mouth was a blue wound and her dress a great bruise. She drank water from a stream the way Jason had taught her—gently so as not to raise the silt. She drank there with a porcupine who bristled and swaggered but from the other side. With sky-blue eyes she stared into his, black and beady, until he slushed around and made off.

She was beginning to be brave when she was alone, resourceful, inventive, watchful. She was alert in a milky way of daisies.

When Jason came back, it was always with some food. Sibbi was glad to see him as she was glad to see the sun rise, because it was reliable, consistent, the act of returning. He told her a little about his day. Now they were whole stories, not the disjointed pieces of his earlier telling. She listened and ate hungrily. She told him no tales because hers were all underground and there were no words yet made for them. He found some higher, protected ground and they went to sleep, wrapped together against the common cold of night.

That first winter, Jason found a position with an old couple so far out of the way they themselves didn't know for sure where they were on the map. They would house and feed him and his sister in return for most of the chores. However they were not well off—they'd have to make do. No-one came to see them anymore, all their sons and daughters buried or far gone. They got no letters, received no news. They couldn't remember the names of all their children. Jason was worried they would die before spring.

Sibbi sat in wonder in the unsteady shadow of extreme age. She stood at the woman's lap and stared at her carved face, her skin like folded velvet as soft as a baby's. She watched in fascination the old woman's hands work wool and scraps with a knowledge separate from her brain. She called Sibbi Rachel, Una, Sarah and her baby. She found a trunk full of worn-out children's clothes and dressed Sibbi in a rainbow of dresses. Sibbi pranced like a plumed pony on a carousel.

Jason spent the winter in an eerie, sullen silence and worked hard, still not his own man. It was a roof over their heads, a fire and food. The old man seemed to visibly shrink before Jason's eyes, sitting on the day-bed in the kitchen, in the winter sun, his arms resting on his emaciated thighs, his hands hung down like hay forks between his knees. He did not talk at all anymore. His wife understood him as a mother does her babies, but Jason did not.

The land began preparing for winter: hedges of thorn, flowers dead, grasses laid low on the contours of the earth, shrivelled into the coarse irregularities of the ground. Rock stood out harsh in the sun and glistened cold in the fall rains. The dark and the cold closed in, as ice conceals a pond until it is gone. When the snow came in the wind it was the only light, without shape or substance; it was the only sound, the wind in the snow. All memory of the land was lost in the present moment. Snow and winter light sifted into all crannies of being, stifled all the senses.

Inside the house the four people sat like burnt-out stars, like black holes in the ends of the universe, their clothes wrapped round them like blankets made of lead-grey snow. In the middle of the bleached planked floor stood the black stove, whispering ashes and a wreath of pale insubstantial warmth, like a faraway sun. There wasn't much difference between day and night. Dawn could as easily close into dark as open into light. The ice thickened on the pond; heartbeats of toads slowed to almost nothing in the still mud near the bottom.

The old woman made an unexpected appearance one time, as if to flap her wings to rid them of the snow. She began to laugh. First it was a small chuckle that bubbled foam from her lips, then it grew and grew. She laughed until tears rolled down her reddened cheeks; she laughed for the sleigh-rides of her childhood, the summer haystacks in bright gold barns, she laughed for the babies she had borne; she laughed for all the love she had seen in seasons of green and open flowers.

The winter was as long as a wolf's wail in a moonbeam on a hill.

When the earth cracked open and the birds returned, Jason set the old couple's field with Sibbi helping him. She sat on her heels and put the seeds in the furrows, then covered them up and patted the dirt down on top with her open flat hands. The old man came out, bent like a dead vine on a pole. He twitched his white-whiskered chin and gave Jason the greying bag-of-bones horse from the barn. Jason hitched it up to his cart, put their belongings into it and led it off up the road. Only Sibbi said goodbye to the woman and kissed her satin cheek. They were sad to see each other go. She gave Sibbi some of the dresses, a shawl, and tied her hair back with a piece of blue velvet ribbon to match her eyes.

Because they were moving again after so long that Sibbi had quite forgotten why, she asked him again.

"Just a while longer now. I'm going to work and make enough money to buy some sheep and we'll find a place where I can build us a house, how about that?"

"Okay," said her small voice, hanging onto belief with

deliberate care.

And indeed, as the snow melted, even in the deep recesses of the woods, they did arrive at the end of the road. Something in the strong forest, the hill-formed meadows and the beginnings of the sea, startled Jason out of his compulsion to follow the open road. It was a fine challenging spring day, vibrant and swift, an immense placid blue sky, the sea turned turquoise, the hills laid new in fragile lettuce green and the forest, half newly budded with soft leaf-casings ready to split, half evergreens with lime-green stems of new growth.

When he stopped the old horse and went to his head, Sibbi knew they would try to stay where they were. She jumped down from the cart and ran to Jason. She put her hand on his.

"Here?"

"Yes, it looks like it's mostly fishing so the hills must be empty."

"Here are you going to make me a home?"

"Yes, a home."

Jason kept his word. He approached the village on his best behaviour and with his most handsome smile. He told the curious the bare truth, that his parents had died and he was looking for a new place since there was nothing left behind. There was a good natural meadow up over the bluff, he was told. It was nobody's. They went and looked. To get there they followed the road that ran out the other end of town, past an old stone schoolhouse. The road ended shortly after and they had to climb up through the forest to the top of the bluff, then over to the other side. The trees ended abruptly and they broke into sun and grass. The hill had a flat top for a cabin and nearby a springing stream. The hill then took a deep slip into a broad valley. Sibbi went and stood close to Jason; she put her hand in his and looked from his face to the valley and back again. There was a deep broad hush, the sea sounds faint, changed in coming through the trees. It was protected here, warm and private. They stood between the bowls of blue sky and green valley with a dark green rim of trees.

Sibbi shouted, possessed by this chosen place, but she was painfully shy in the village. She pressed her knuckles white holding onto Jason, by hand or flapping coat-tail. She had no smile there, no frown, just watched with the face of an owl. Up on the hill she worked hard alongside Jason, in her fashion, holding him, or the ladder or nails. He worked with an amazing fierce eagle strength. The sun glinted off the blue-black of his hair, sank deep into his skin until he was two halves, a brown top and white bottom. The muscles rippled down his arms and across his back.

He put up a lean-to and they lived like gypsies in the marvelous summer sun. He cut thick trees and shaped them into corner posts with his axe. He dug deep holes to bed-rock and poured cement into them, around the posts. He nailed up cross-pieces and braces until an ox could not have pulled it down. He laid a floor. He went into the forest for more logs; the horse dragged them out one by one. Jason took off the bark with the axe, leaving them round and creamy white. He laid the logs one by one on top of each other, fitting their notched ends together. The sides rose until it looked like a box. When they were about six feet high he sawed down and made a window overlooking the meadow. He and Sibbi stood inside on the plank floor and looked out the empty hole. The inside was filled with sun and there was no door. Sibbi ran around inside pressing on the walls, pushing herself off, back into the small room. It smelt clean and woody. Jason lifted her out the window and sawed a door hole in the south wall, where the sun could come in. Sibbi went in and out several times and asked Jason to build a step there for her.

Though the building was plain and practical, Jason spent

61

himself on the fireplace. It spread across half the end wall and was made of rough-hewn stones set together in cement. It would be impervious to weather and the stone would hold the heat long after the embers had died out. The fireplace would impose itself on the cabin as his mother's old drum stove never had. He built in a baking oven and left holes drilled for wrought-iron fixtures. He laid a brick apron in front raised above the floor with a place beneath for logs to dry out. It was a masterpiece; he would be able to sit and watch the whole being of a fire he had created, its colour, its warmth, its security and secret memory of energy released to keep him.

He laid more logs until the walls were about seven feet high. Then he laid beams across the top and put on the peaked roof frame. He bought shingles for the roof so the snows would slide off, and oakum from the fishermen to caulk between the logs. He made a window-frame but had to wait for a piece of glass; in the meantime he made shutters. Last was the door; he drilled a hole for the latch, slipped it through, and shut the door with them inside. It was dark: Jason was pleased and waited for the next rain.

When the sky darkened one afternoon and the air was clinging to the clouds, Jason and Sibbi dragged their belongings from the lean-to and put the horse under it. They just got inside the cabin when the hush was broken and it began to rain. They sat on boxes. The door was latched, the window shuttered. They listened and watched for leaks. There didn't seem to be any so Jason could say, "Well, here's our house, Sibbi," and the words echoed in the empty room.

She moved apart, sensing that he wanted to sit alone, put her arms around herself, held onto herself. She loved the house already, its brown raw-bark walls, the shape of the vaulted roof, the window opening to the meadow, but it was not as warm as skin, as holding his hand would have been. It was the end of August again.

Sibbi became a housewife while Jason went to work for various people in the village every day. She picked a bunch of straw-flowers and clover, put them in a cup on the saw-horse table in the middle of the room. She swept the floor daily. She kicked the straw mattress on the floor into some sort of shape and tried to smooth the blankets over the lumpy surface. She tucked the long bench under the table and rearranged the boxes that held supplies. In one lay her clothes folded and piled on top of each other. She wore a path to the stream going back and forth for water for she could only carry a third of a bucket at a time.

She was not as idle in these days of being alone as she had been before. In the meadow she encountered the snake, the porcupine, the squirrel and the deer. Breathless, she met the fawn with its spots almost gone, but young enough not to be afraid of her. Sibbi wished she had liquid brown eyes like the fawn.

The trees were all of one colour at first, then gently yellow began to spread through the leaves, then a rash of red came up through the forest. The nights were cold; Sibbi put a blanket on the old horse and fed him a piece of sugar through his white-whiskered muzzle. He slobbered contentedly, the froth dripping from his mouth. Jason took the horse with him one morning and when he came back he was alone. Sibbi looked anxiously around, but there was no horse anywhere. Jason patted her head, then opened his jacket. Sibbi's eyes and mouth both made a round O. There was a puppy with a short blunt face, all nose and wet eyes. Sibbi took it out of his jacket, lifting it under the front legs. The puppy yelped and scratched the air. Quickly she drew it to her breast, cradling it, covering it with her arms and hands, and bending her face into the silky fur.

"Is this your dog?" she asked, hoping.

"Yes, it's a dog to keep the sheep."

"Is it a pet too?"

63

"No."

But Sibbi hugged the puppy tighter. She made a bed for it with a dress that was too small for her and when they went to sleep she had her hand under the puppy's head.

The first winter was difficult. The cabin held a trial of repairs against the ravages of fierce winds that blew up from the valley. On hard crisp blue-white days, Jason went into the woods alone to chop the dry brittle trees that would be next winter's supply of wood. He built a sleigh and pulled the logs back to the lean-to. There wasn't a great deal to eat, for they had no garden and Jason was saving money for his sheep. In the fitful firelight he trained the puppy until it was his dog as he had said, despite the affection Sibbi lavished on it whenever she could. She was learning to sustain herself in winter as well as summer—alone—for Jason sank into himself whenever he wasn't working. Despite his craving for domesticity, for home and hearth, he was restive in its cage and in the cave of his own mind. His memory didn't flicker on top of the fire in the fragile illusive colour of flame. It seethed gold-grey in the turmoil of hot ashes beneath.

For the first time they were alone together. They sat back to back and this is the way they were alone. Sibbi picked pieces of straw out of the bed or pushed them back in.

Jason built things indoors. He laid a loft across the beams at one end, for storage space. He built a proper bed with four posts, pieces along to hold it together, holes drilled in the planks and heavy rope criss-crossed on which to lay the mattress. He bought an old trunk with leather hinges and rounded top and Sibbi packed away their clothes. He put shelves on the wall too high for her to reach, but it didn't matter; they had so little the shelves were empty. He built a cupboard to hold their two plates, cups, utensils, the cooking pot and frying pan. Two buckets on the floor served, one for water, the other to wash in. There were no rugs on the floor. There were three heavy, worn blankets on the bed and they rolled up in them to keep out the drafts. Jason let the puppy sleep between them because he was warm. They wore their clothes to bed. Snow seeped in the split between the shutters and didn't melt overnight. Jason left Sibbi in bed until he had built the fire in the mornings. He taught her how to boil potatoes, make corn-meal porridge, cook wild game he had shot. He showed her how to render the fat out of birds and venison by boiling. She was so attentive; she so loved him then, in wonder at what he knew and because he was attending to her, watching her when she tried something, covering her hand with his.

Sometimes she was brave enough to break into his silence. "Jason, will you tell me a story, when you feel like it, about when you were small like me and with mother?"

"No, not with her." She had become his possession totally, privately and he didn't want to share her even with his own flesh. "But I'll tell you about what I did. You know I always worked hard—did a man's work long before I was a man. . . ."

"Didn't you ever play?" From Sibbi who didn't seem to be doing much playing either now.

"No, not really, I was alone a lot with Mother, and I worked, but we never had much. . ."

Sibbi was bored with the story, but grateful for the words. He talked at her; the slippery words caressing her ears with sound, haunting her senses like the wail of the loon, hooting at her in the night of white owls. She learned new words and to use them told stories to herself from imagination and her own meagre memory. When daylight was gone there was only night and the fire. Night left to sort out the last day. Dreams to order the next day. She survived.

Spring came in the first dawn of the whole world. They emerged from the cold damp pit into the unremembered lightness of the earth uncovered. Sibbi took off her boots, which were too small, and ran over the woolly grass barefoot. Jason would take her old boots to the village next fall to trade for a new pair, when her feet had finished their summer growing.

There was still snow in the deep woods and hollows when Jason went off with his dog to have it trained to the sheep. He came back in the evening and went immediately to bed; he had to be up early and to work, building a three-sided shelter for the sheep and a fence to enclose a yard for them until they knew their home. The shelter was constructed on a high mound, its open side facing the trees so it would have good ventilation, yet be protected. He built a low sturdy stump fence that even a crush of sheep couldn't break. It led out and around from the shelter and opened into a big loop down the hill. He built another separate paddock, small and square, in which the ram could rest. He built a hay shed on four poles with a floor above the ground, air space between the boards on the sides and a teepee roof with long overhanging eaves on all sides. He would buy hay and straw from the farms.

Jason sat on the stoop, in the sun, emptied his tin of money onto the step. Sibbi had never seen it all before, so much there was, paper and coins. He put it into a small leather pouch, put on his plaid wool shirt and went off to fetch the dog and buy the sheep, now that everything was ready for their arrival. He would be gone for a week, learning how to work the dog with them. He scratched the days in a log for Sibbi to count, to mark them off one by one.

She was alone again. She was seven years old. In the daylight she leaned into the chill fresh winds. In the night she hid under the covers thinking about the lambs she could love.

One morning Sibbi followed the orange-bellied gulls when they wheeled back from the meadow, over the bluff to the sea. The forest was clear of mist, the trees tall, silent, working inside to put out new leaves, the buds oozing sap. Beneath them, mayflowers winked white blossoms and ferns still furled on their stalk stood up out of the leaf-mould. Shapelessness gave way to shadow and substance as the sun laid its light on the land. The spurt of a songbird's call in the woods gave way to the long hoarse-throated crows and gulls who flapped and rode the thermals down the seaside of the bluff.

She couldn't even look at the sea; she raised her arm to her forehead because of the sun like fire on the water. The mist simmered like steam in the cove. She couldn't find any footsteps in the path as she made her way down.

She went into the shadow of the schoolhouse and peeked in the open window. There was a man asleep, white sheets and a multicoloured quilt on the bed; a rug on the floor and a picture of a family in a thin gold frame on a dresser. She went to another window and saw another room with a fire-place, a stove, inside pump and sink, a padded chair and more pictures. She stuck her head in the window and looked at the bookcase. She knew what they were but had never seen so many together. If she had been able to stretch enough, the temptation might have been too great; but the books were out of reach. She pushed herself back, a fox retreating into the thicket of alders. Overhead a buckshot explosion of gulls leaped out of the cliff, black and white in the blueing air, catching the sun here and there on their bodies, their wing-beats overwhelming the waves. She ran out of the schoolyard, reaching, swirling as purposelessly as the first strong rise of the gulls. Her flight dazzled the earthbound stones, her dress billowed out. The gulls beck-oned and she followed their freedom with her fingers, touch-ing the wind they made in the morning. Then she lit again in the grass, on the earth and the gulls went their own way. Sibbi breathed deeply to press back the ache for something lost.

67

The gulls swung out over the water into the sun and were gone. She clutched her skirt with ramrod-straight arms, eyes closed, waiting for gravity to pull down hard enough on her legs so she could walk. Or run off atop the bluff away from the village; she ran with the skill of a deer, manœuvring the sing-song path. Out of the corner of her eye she watched her shadow streaming along, as long as a scythe across the grass.

She ran until her breath gave out and the land was turning to stone. Until the grass seemed uneasy, bleached and stiffened with salt spray. It cut her ankles because if it would not yield to the sea it wouldn't even notice her skin. Here the rocks were peeling with flakes of white lichen. The tiny umbrella flowers of yellowy-green samphire hung on with the rough scrub evergreen juniper. She came over a small rise. And there, coming out of the ground against the pearly blue sky, were dead white trees, small, naked as bone, ignored, too thin to beat down, petrified by salt and sun. At first they frightened her, but then she approached one, fascinated, touched the smooth pale branch and rubbed it until the oil in her skin made it shiny, the friction warm. She lay back on the grass until all she could see was the tree in the sky, as if its shape had fallen through the blue into some other place.

As the sun arched over her head its heat and light forced her eyelids tighter and tighter shut until she unconsciously rolled over on her side and slept in the easy curled shape of a cat.

It was just past mid-morning, when the day was fully awake, that Morgan decided to walk out to the land's end. In a green schoolbag he carried a book of poetry, a lunch of bread and cheese, and a bottle of wine. Over his arm, because it was getting hot, he carried a coarsely woven blanket. His boots crunched steadily on the grass and lichen. When he climbed the last hump of land he was startled to see a limp still form lying there. He put down his packet and bent as if to sniff at her. The wind had mixed the grass with her dishevelled hair and she was breathing. He put his hand on her shoulder. "Missy, hey Missy, wake up." Sibbi woke up fast enough but could hardly move her sun-salted bones. She scrambled awkwardly and squinted into the dark-in-shadow brand-new face.

"Are you okay?" he asked, crouched opposite her.

"Do you belong here?" Because she was still half asleep and he was part of her forgotten dreams.

"Well yes, I suppose so. D'you?"

"I just came here." And she patted the ground.

"It's okay to come here, I came too, just now, and found you."

"Found." Not a question, just repeating his word.

"Yes, I found you, here, sleeping." Patiently amused.

"I was asleep." A statement of fact, the only thing she was absolutely sure about.

Morgan smiled, "I think you still are."

"I don't know who you are."

"My name is Morgan."

"I know who you are, I saw you asleep in the bed on the white sheets."

"You did!" Startled.

She nodded with emphasis. "Yes, I did."

"And when did you see me asleep?"

"Today, through the window. It was open."

She's without guile, he thought. "Have you visited before?"

"No. This is the first time I've come out." She seemed to shrink slightly.

"May I ask who you are?"

"I am. . . well, my name is Sibbi." And she stretched her tongue down her chin to its outermost point, then flipped it back in.

"Where do you live?"

"In the house on top of the hill and it's all logs and. . . and I'm all alone." Eyes large and mysterious.

"Are you always alone?"

She shook her head. Her lips made a fist that crinkled her nose.

"Are you alone all day today?"

"Yes," her eyes smiled, "I am today."

Morgan rolled back and sat down.

"I'm going to have a picnic, would you like to join me?"

"I can go away."

"I'm sure you can, but would you like to stay?"

She bent her head now that she was awake, her shyness gone in the broad hot sunlight. "Okay."

Morgan shook open the blanket on the grass. It looked like their straw-filled mattress. He opened the bag and took out bread, cheese, knife and wine.

Sibbi eyed the food. "I'm already hungry," she said.

"Are you!" He laughed out loud. "Well, then we should eat now, before the cheese melts." He cut off hunks of bread and the sweating cheese. Sibbi took her piece and ate it.

"Do you like wine?"

"I never had it."

"Here, only don't take too much." She took a little sip and washed down the bread.

"It ruins the taste of the cheese." She took another wedge of crust.

Morgan ate and drank slowly, looking out to sea for a long time, while Sibbi stared mostly at his face. She drank in the newness of another human being, the way an animal unabashedly absorbs the being of its new keeper. The headland wind blew his thick brown hair away from his face, his high brow. He had heavy eyebrows and brown eyes, liquid like a fawn. His lips were mobile, they ate food and spoke words with an ease she hadn't seen before. He seemed

70

to her domestic, innocent of the axe and stone, yet open to the other place, held brooding in the head.

When they were both finished eating Morgan reached into his bag again.

"May I read you something?"

"Read?"

He was rather taken aback, she said it so loudly, startled.

"Yes, from this book I brought. I was going to read to myself but now since you're my company, I thought you might like to listen."

She sat up, on the brink of something, every fibre inside as taut as tinsel. Her whole being, all her senses pinpointed themselves in spite of herself on the simple act of his taking the book into his hand and opening it to expose the creamy pages splattered with print. She was hovering like a moth before the flame.

Morgan said "Spring," but he was not saying it out of his own head, he was reading.

Nothing is so beautiful as Spring—
    When weeds, in wheels, shoot long and lovely and
        lush;
    Thrush's eggs look little low heavens, and thrush
Through the echoing timber does so rinse and wring
The ear, it strikes like lightnings to hear him sing;
    The glassy pear tree leaves and blooms, they brush
    The descending blue; that blue is all in a rush
With richness; the racing lambs too have fair their fling.

What is all this juice and all this joy?
    A strain of the earth's sweet being in the beginning
In Eden garden. Have, get, before it cloy,
    Before it cloud, Christ, lord, and sour with sinning,
Innocent mind and Mayday in girl and boy,
    Most, O maid's child, thy choice and worthy the winning.

"Again," she said.

5

It is the same land, tumbled in full-leafed trees, rolled in rough grass, yawning in wind-formed waves until it is snapped off by the rise of a cliff, a ragged rock-slice into the everlasting Atlantic, over that last defiance of earth. Gulls with mist and sun-bleached backs and wings, spread like ice crystals growing on the deep window surface of the sea. Their cries rise up the cliff through the smell of parched pine and patchy grass. The morning feels like silk.

Alone in an opaque cocoon, beaten down, grey, Sibbi sat on the floor with only the faintest sounds reaching her. It didn't matter if her eyes were open or closed, the same un-identifiable objects coalesced momentarily, then lost their substance. She kept her precarious balance by rocking back and forth to the loud rhythm of her beating heart. Her body was made of concrete; there was the vague knowledge some-where that she must not lie down or she would be sucked into the quicksand of whatever was underneath her.

Morgan had to dress her that morning, folding her limp limbs this way and that to fit them in the chemise and sleeve-less jumper. The only time she seemed to resist him was when he laced a pair of canvas shoes on her feet. He had to spoon-feed her some hot porridge. "Oh, Sibbi, why do you come and go so?" And: "Where are you today Sibbi? In what darkness?" Or: "Under what cloud are you fighting today? Or are you just resting?" For her skin was cool.

Morgan slung his threadbare bag over one shoulder and took Sibbi's hand in his. "Come on, we're going to try the land's end today."

Two long lean shadows lay up the hill, running with the ease of the shadow of a cloud, across the slopes. The mist was slipping in invisible ribbons, evaporating in the hot sun. Sibbi caught a glimpse of it as shards of glass or ice slicing something softly green.

He found them a place beneath the bleached short spires of the stripped trees, laid his blanket on the rough hummocky grass and sat her down, then himself. She put her arms out and swung once around as if to see if there were any stops. The fact that there were not didn't seem to bother her. She furled her arms around herself as unopened leaves hug the stem. Morgan reached over and settled the straw hat more firmly on her head. Her hair stuck out in little wisps from under the band, framing a face that melted into a strange slackness, though youth and thinness held it together.

Morgan lay down on his stomach and read his book while Sibbi rocked to and fro behind him. He read and fought sleepiness in the stunning sun until it was nearly noon. Then he pulled the bag out from under one corner of the blanket and took out a lunch of vine-ripened tomatoes, hard-boiled eggs, bread, cured ham, wine for himself and a jug of milk for her. He put a piece of ham into her hand, folded her fingers around it and waited. Then he put her hand to her face and finally she began to eat the meat out of her fist. Morgan was suddenly very tired. He had thought it would be a good idea to come here, to take her into the hills she might remember. To bring her back to where they first crossed paths long, long ago. But today she was only a leaf, cool, dry, apart, at the end of somewhere, in a shade he couldn't fathom.

He folded up his things and his expectations and took her home.

The starch of fall came first in the winds blowing out of the north where winter was already driving storms. The earth turned around so the sun sought new angles and shorter hours in the sky. Morgan measured Sibbi with his eye and went into the village to buy her a warm coat at the second-hand shop. He went to the Post Office; there were no letters for him. He thought about giving up, about getting Sibbi dressed, her satchel packed, and taking her down to the bus-stop, going with her to the train and putting her into someone's hands to take to the city, to the asylum. If only she would do one thing that would give him confidence or hope that this was all worth while, that it wasn't a terrible waste of time and energy. He read: "There are some children who are so damaged that they are hopeless in the present state of our knowledge; if we knew more, if we only knew. . . but do not give up until your ingenuity and instinct totally fail or are about to be submerged, hence would be of no use to anyone else. . . ." He read it again. His instinct was to force her, to shake that covering off, to squeeze some sound out of her. She had cried once; she had touched him once, she could do it again. She was a strong child, though broken somewhere. Unless he felt her he couldn't find out where. As he walked home with her parcel under his arm, the wind matched his own energy. It was crisp and new from the snow, from the hard clear form of the ice. The fascination of order, pattern and symmetry. His perseverance, his will to endure fire and survive.

When he got home, he put the package on the table and undid the string. He stood Sibbi up and put the coat on her. He did up the buttons and shook it a bit to be sure it fit properly. He took the coat off her and hung it up. She just stood there all the time it took him to remake the fire, cook a supper and eat it and wash up the few dishes. The sun ceased coming in the windows at all, could only be seen frosting the sky. Morgan shut the door against the chill, stirred the fire and stood watching it. If there was wind outside it could always be seen and felt here in the flame. So now the wind wandered, cloaked in orange, burrowing in the live ash.

Morgan turned on Sibbi, stood over her. He took her face in his hands, lifted it, his palms under her knife-sharp chin. He reached up with his thumbs and pulled back her eyelids. She felt the light change behind her eyes. Her gaze was hollow. He dropped her head and it nodded listlessly. He snatched her hand up, opened it, rubbed it until it stayed open. He took an apple from the bowl on the table and put it into her hand, folded her fingers over it.

"Can you feel that, Sibbi? It's an apple, cool and red. . . ."

He snatched it away, crumpled a piece of paper into a ball and put that in her waiting hand. "And that, paper. . . ."

He dragged her to the edge of the table, rubbed her hand on the wood, on the edge, on the chair cushion, the wall, the window, the pump handle, the basin, a pot, a dish, a cup, the damp towel lying in a heap on the counter, the door-knob, the blanket on her bed. He drew a piece of string through her fingers, laid a spoon on them, pressed the tines of a fork on her skin. He took both her hands and closed them around her own skirt, made her squeeze the flannel, pull on it. He named and described each object.

He took her hands and put them open on his own shirt.

"This is me, Sibbi, damn it, I'm here." He covered her hands with one of his and took the other to lift her chin. "Do you feel it? Another heart than yours? Wake up!" he shouted. She blinked involuntarily at the sound. He lifted her hand to his cheek, where he had a day-old beard, and desperately rubbed her lizard-like hand back and forth. Then slid it down over his mouth, held it there and panted into the rubbery cup. Her other hand remained over his heart. He felt it press, then seem to gain strength, searching his chest, the fingers travelling over the layers of muscles, cautiously following the bones. He held dead still while she found his heart-beat. Her breath held in her throat. Her fingers crawled upward through the twin points of his collar bones, ever so lightly onto his throat. He breathed

75

into her hand again while her other came to rest as gently as a lover's on the pulse in his throat. She rested her thumb on the other side and felt the confusion of two pulses; she didn't know if she was losing her own or gaining his. Her other hand came alive between his mouth and palm, exploring, straining as a blade of wheat might strain to understand the sun.

Morgan didn't know what to do in this silence, this smooth grey pond of water he was under without his kind of air, while he could feel the current of her coming. Then he felt her slide to one side, like a stream around a stone. Her hands lifted, leaving a vacuum between them. He grabbed at her, her indifference, her drifting away. This time he would hold onto the tail of sunlight or moonlight if he had to chase it clear over the horizon. Before he could let her go he must have some sign from her eyes, some sliver of recognition between the blinds of her vision.

"Wake up," he tried again, loud, his hands loud on the bones of her shoulders, shaking her. He took her around the waist and hurried her outside onto the cold sharp grass, into the strong liquid wind full of snow that made the trees shiver and the leaves curl. The wind sounded here and there in the depths of the trees. The moon was a white round hole in the black sky. It was alone, haloed; there were no stars. When he felt her shiver he took her over to the well. He drew up a bucket of ice-cold water from under the fish. He set the bucket on the ground and dunked her hands into it. She tried to pull them out. He held them down and swished them around, then lifted them to her face. She felt the icy-cold tentacles on her eyes, nose and mouth. He took her hands and put them to his own face. He watched. Her forehead wrinkled at the difference of cold and warmth. She felt the pads of her fingers warm up when they touched his skin.

"Oh Sibbi, admit it with your eyes, admit it, admit me."

76

So she lifted up her head of her own accord and saw him day old in the grey-white second-hand light of the moon.

"That's my girl!" he exclaimed. He sat down on the damp edge of the well, turned her around and held her against him in relief.

Sibbi felt the transition, the release of a pressure that had made her skin tingle, a peace that turned the grey acrid smoke into soft silver. The layer of solid cold that lodged perpetually just under her skin melted a little and let her feel the pattern of something outside herself.

With Morgan himself again the children brightened in class. The village folk remarked that they were glad to see the change because, charitable and humane as his efforts were with the little girl who was dumb as a post, they could not, in all fairness to their own children, let him neglect them. He tried once again to let them share with him his small triumph, but they weren't really interested. He spent an evening in a council meeting to reassure everyone and to re-establish himself in the world of men he had so little time for. To be reminded himself of the physical world he pitched in on a barn-raising and was stiff and sore for days. He drank corn whisky until he laughed so hard he shook his brains into a better order in his head, and his heart found a release that was splendid and strengthening. He walked home from the barn-raising, not yet sore, and sang the choruses of college songs to the night.

He woke Sibbi when he got home. The sight of her did not totally sober him up. "Well Sibbi, old girl, see this face, this worked-out body; well, some day you'll be able to do the same." That took real effort. He put his head down; it wasn't exactly what he'd had in mind, but it would do. He chucked her under the chin before covering her up again.

While the spirit was strong and the flesh recovering, he began to work on her as on a painting. He set her up on the easel of a chair, her hands on the table. He filled her mind with words, describing the food she was eating, sponging her incipient senses. After supper he put objects in front of her and laid her hands on them. He talked to her, he touched her when she couldn't feel it. He laid her head on a sweet-grass mat and crushed mint leaves under her nose. Sometimes her eyes flickered. He exposed the obdurate grey canvas of her body to colours, textures and sounds.

Once she saw him coming. She had been at rest in the vast stretching leaden plains and something fell in, cut the veil, opened a clean wound to the world. He came like lightning and it was too sudden. She jumped up, fled to her bed, clutched her pillow across her stomach. Raising her arm to ward him off, she put her elbow through the window glass. There was no pain in the lacerations, only the blood was horrible, the desperate colour, dripping red on the sheets and blanket. She gave herself up to Morgan to mend the colour. He wondered that she didn't cry, for the cuts were severe. On her face there was only an expression of disgust and distress.

He had changed the sheets right away, but one night she had a dream about the blood. She ran her fingers up and down her ribs and up under her breasts. When Morgan awoke in the middle of the night it was to a peculiar thumping noise, muffled, yet solid, unyielding. He got up by moonlight. Sibbi was sitting up in her bed, silhouetted against the windows. She had made steel fists of both hands and was methodically beating her outstretched thighs.

"Stop it. You're hurting yourself." He closed his hands over hers. Her strength was almost superhuman; his muscles trembled with the effort it took to hold her hands. He was so used to her face he thought he could see a nuance of expression, or was it only the moon shadows? She leaned her head back and pulled her face into an expression that said, gently and ever so quietly, "Oh, what do you know."

"In the meantime, Sibbi, until you can tell me what I need

to know, I'll blunder into your world. I can only try, the way I ask you to." She hung her head, the cold coming back under her skin.

In the morning light, Morgan inspected her thighs. She'd succeeded in raising a welter of bruises. The colour was beginning to come like oil spreading on mud. She saw them herself and Morgan caught her looking at his face as he bent over her.

"Well?" he said roughly.

She reached down and covered herself. But she was not hidden. She had felt shame and it had melted the cold, which didn't come back as surely as before, but hovered like slush on her edges. She sat at the table when Morgan went to class. She put her hands on the wood and felt that it was different from her own skin. Though her fingers moved uneasily she kept them there. The room was full of objects, all shades of slate and cinder, but they were fixed, did not float or disappear. The air was hot and muggy; she could smell wood ash and, from the ash-tray in front of her on the table, the smell of stale pipe tobacco. The window was open; she heard the gentling breeze in the trees and saw two pale leaves float by. At the back of her head she heard the murmur of voices. Finally she felt surprise because she wasn't really afraid. All these things were just there, demanding nothing from her, allowing her space. She felt the movement, the cycle of a whole day without descents into darkness. She was thankful.

6

There were no days left on the log. Sibbi sat scratching termite trails into the soft wood for a while, then she took it inside and burned it. Jason was either late or not coming back at all. She cleaned up the mess she had made in a week

79

inside the cabin; picked mayflowers out of the snow in the woods' deepest hollows and dandelions out of the field, put them in a cup on the table. She danced herself a little jig out the door, across the path to the sheep shed, where there still was no sheep smell. Yet. She climbed onto the fence and dangled there—waiting.

Darkness was imminent when she heard the holler up the hill. "Open the gate Sibbi, open the gate." She leapt up, ran to the fence and opened it wide. There was Jason struggling in a foam of white, hanging on for dear life to a huge ewe who was certainly not used to the leash he held her with. The dog wasn't being very serious either. He leaped, darted, sank all of a sudden with only his tail up in the air, waving rhythmically back and forth until he exploded up again, ears flapping crazily. Sibbi held it as long as she could, then bent double with laughter, hiding behind the gate until she could regain control. She peered out through her fingers. Jason's face was livid with frustration. The ewe dug her four feet into the grass and leaned backward. Jason sunk his hands up to the wrists in wool and heaved her bodily into the paddock. When she was finally tied to a post well inside, he climbed out and chased the dog who chased the rest of the sheep everywhere but through the gate.

"Goddamned dog, come here," he shouted until the dog stopped in mid-stride and looked up happily. "Come here, you." And down went the dog's head into the grass as he slunk nearer, as near as he dared. Jason gave him a healthy swat on the rump, then gathered him up and walked gently around the stragglers, herding them toward the gate. When they saw the tethered sheep they tried to reach her and were soon running in clumps around the outside of the fence. Patiently Jason rounded them up and drove them into the pen. Once inside they started to bleat piteously, as if injured.

"Close the gate, Sibbi, wherever you are." She did so while he gathered up the last small stray and unceremoniously dumped it inside. The dog came all awag to Sibbi, who rubbed his back, her fingers in his thick hair. She looked into the pen where the sheep billowed like captured clouds.

A while later she asked, "Do you like them, Jason?" But he didn't like them, he didn't even answer. She made him something to eat, for he was hungry. Then he slept for ten hours. She soon forgot to tell him about her days alone. She hunched down on her heels by the side of the bed and supported herself on her elbows, staring at him asleep, dreamless. The dog lay heavily in front of the fire, some of the disgrace gone now that his master was sleeping.

Jason's mouth was slack with sleep. Instead of fineness, softness showing through in this unprotected condition, he looked like a great piece of mute machinery that should be in constant motion. Sibbi touched his arm, then stood up, turned around and sat on the piece of wood that underlay the mattress. That way he couldn't feel her. She didn't look at him anymore. She whispered.

"Jason, I did do everything you told me to. . . ." The dog thumped his tail on the floor in his sleep. "Jason, I went over the bluff to the sea, only once, and do you know what happened?" The firelight made a question mark on the wall.

"Well, this man found me and woke me up. We had a picnic just like we used to have on the road. Then d'you know what?" But the fire was bored and the dog asleep. "He had a book and he read me something out of the book." She shivered, her bottom was going to sleep on the board. "Jason, I want to learn to read, I want to. . . . He said he was the schoolmaster. . . . I want to go to school. . . ."

Nothing answered.

The next morning at breakfast: "Jason, I want to go to school."

"No, not yet, there's too much to do here. School can wait."

And the morning after. "Jason, I want to learn to read."

"I'll teach you how to read sometime."

Again. "Jason, I want. . . ."

"No, I told you. You've got things to do here, now that's final. There's no school in summer anyway, so forget it for now." She put her spoon angrily into her porridge. Jason looked at her hard for the first time in a long while. He didn't seem to remember her very well. Her reference to him was very slight. The volume of his life was so physical he often forgot her except when he needed her. That she should want anything, be separate in any way, was as foreign to him now as it had ever been. Rarely did he have the inclination to touch her reality with his. The time into which he was stolen was bitter tasting. Jason was not a stupid man, but he did not know he was starving. Those histories that were left underneath became increasingly hard to find. He was in danger of not being able to recognize them. When he looked at Sibbi and saw her, he was putting his feet into a swamp.

There was little need to slow down, or time to take a backward glance that summer. The dog stopped playing with the sheep and learned to manage them tolerably well when let loose over the springing pastures. Having been bred late the ewes didn't lamb until the first week in June. They took all week to do it. Mercifully the weather held dry and warm through the long nights when the lamps flickered yellow like fireflies in the long grass. The ewes were all young and many needed help with their firstborn. One was so surprised by the piece of herself lying limp by her side that Jason had to tie her up and hand-milk her swollen udder into the lamb's mouth. Ten sheep turned into twenty and, among them, a male was born who would sire a future flock.

The dog was left in the cabin to howl with frustration, but Sibbi was dragged willingly out at midnight to wait and watch. In the moonlight, the blood on the lambs was blue, their skin silver. It was the most royal thing she had ever seen.

That summer Sibbi was happy because she was able to work side by side with Jason. She didn't actually know the difference yet, that they were never together, if indeed that was possible. Simply side by side, it was enough when embroidered by her imagination. She looked at him with admiration for his ability to do things, to get along, to know what to do, how and when; she felt pride in being at his side. Allowed there and needed, the reasons blurred. It didn't matter; she didn't seek the elusive absolutes that so antagonized Jason. The uplands were lush and wild with striped bees, yellow pollen and owls; the sheep were wilful, but she had worn footpaths. She was known. Her feet were known on the ground, in the garden; her hands were known by the bodies of the sheep and the soil, her hair known by the sun, her voice known by the wind.

Summer, the wilderness accepted every shape she made, every intrusion, every mistake. It did not violate her green centre. It let her be, superb, innocent.

It was winter that she remembered. In winter, as at sea at night, there was no way of telling where the land was. She could only send yearning songs out like doves. The earth darkened. Cold crept into the cracks of the bark while the branches above lost their leaves. They dried and died, then frost got them on the ground. The land shrank; solid, hard, it wouldn't accept rain any more. The sheep huddled, silent in the fold, and watched snow come out of the thin dawn, through their trees. It fell on the hay-shed. The mice burrowed deeper. Sibbi kneeled at the window and poked braids of oakum into the drafty cracks around the edges while the snow settled in upside-down arcs on the frames. The dog came in and shook a blizzard on the floor, then stretched out to dry in front of the fire. The sheep became invisible. The cabin was adrift, alone, of no consequence. Jason tied a rope from the cabin to the shed to the outhouse so they wouldn't get lost. The buildings stood like black hulls, creaking at the end of their moorings, the ropes strung out like snow-covered suspension bridges. The wind shrieked.

When they were shut up in the one small room, Sibbi was even more alone. Jason went into the woods to cut the sere trees. The sound of his axe rang in the air, but it was over a great untraceable distance. He sawed the wood in the yard until the snow was sprinkled with sawdust and his face was red and glistening.

The sheep trod down the snow in their pens as they wandered slowly under the winter sun. When one of the sheep slipped down on a slick of ice and broke its leg, Jason took it behind the house and stuck a knife up under its skull in the back of its brain. He cut off all the wool, rolled the thick piece up and tied it with twine. He hung the carcass up by the hind feet, cut the throat open and let the blood run out into a bucket. He slit open the belly, took out the entrails, which he boiled for the dog, and sawed up the rest for himself and Sibbi. He thought to himself he would get a piglet in the spring to fatten, and perhaps a couple of laying hens.

Jason took two sheep to the village to sell and buy provisions to supplement the meagre stores the garden had yielded in its first year. He bought Sibbi a packet of needles, thread, darning yarn and a paper of pins. He taught her how to sew, a clumsy stitch that her nimble fingers quickly refined. She mended his clothes, put exquisite patches on all the holes, made thick pot-holders from scraps and began fashioning a patchwork quilt from the torn-up squares of her outgrown dresses. Jason paid little attention to her clothing. It wasn't until the seams split or armholes rubbed her raw that he remembered to pick up something larger for her. The memory of two winters ago fluttered before her every time she washed the faded blue ribbon the old woman had given her and hung it near the fire. But one night Jason inadvertently knocked it off the hook and it was instantly burnt up in the flame.

Wood smoke, wet wool, potato water, musty straw, dried footprints, all these smells mixed together, one at a time dominating, then slowly being stirred to the bottom. On quiet, frozen days she opened the door to fill the room with cold expressionless pure snowy air. Otherwise the cabin was closed in to conserve heat.

When chores were done and it was too dark to sew she sat at the edge of the firelight behind Jason. The evening was measured in hardwood logs or the motion of the moon across the sky.

She was stung under the skin until, over the sleeping body of Jason in the night, through the window, she sought the moon and snow-bathed hills, cold and blue, their silence like a truce.

7

Sibbi was shared with another day. The sun shone and she walked upon the earth. Miles and miles. She measured the shadows and wandered in and out of the heat of the sun and the cold of the clouds. She remembered nothing, dreamed nothing. She followed the chant of the wind until day fall.

She was so hungry. She took her plate and began to eat.

"You're hungry." With the appetite of good health, Morgan thought. Between mouthfuls of his own he spoke to her. "You're going to get more hungry too, hungry for action and rest, hungry for life and being alive, hungry for the outside and even for your own memories."

Sibbi spoke with her eyes: *Please don't push me.*

"All in good time, all in your time—as well as I can make it out with as much as you tell me." She seemed to breathe more easily. "You know, I've always believed that human beings have something like a tap-root inside them that goes

85

way down, out of all we know, beyond ourselves as we are now, it remembers us from before, before we were present and accountable. Our link with impulse. When you really cry out, Sibbi, your cry will be filled with sap from that root, with the blood of every beginning."

That evening he put the lamp between them on the table. He sat her down in the chair opposite his. He put a pad of paper in front of her and a pencil in her hand. She laid her head down and watched his hands on the school scribblers, checking, marking, writing messages, turning over the pages to see what was on the other side. Idly she held the pencil between two fingers, tapping it on the paper, then slowly twisted it round so she could write. She listened to the sound the point made as it moved over the paper, but it left no mark. Then she went to sleep.

The next week it rained almost every day. Morgan was oppressed by the four walls of the classroom, as were the children.

"The next fine day, how about a field trip?"

Unanimous chorus of yeas. And they were able to settle down to lower mathematics and ancient history for a few hours.

He tried Sibbi out on the paper every evening that week and every night it was left blank. It frightened him, like emptiness. She would not be hurried. She was part of the earth's most secret things: the roots of a mountain, the breath of a fish, the sound of a prowling cat.

On the day when the white birds, like the fling of a fisherman's net, were in the blue sky and swooping to the surface of the sea, broiling up white water, skimming for scraps, Morgan gathered the children, who were impatient and thrumming alive, stomping feet, *halloes* shouted to each other in excitement over the interminable length of night now past. They pushed each other, made feigned punches at one another's lunch bags. They split into groups, made death-pact promises to sit with one another at lunch time.

"Does everyone have everything?"

"Yes," from half the class. Gasps from the other half who suddenly realized they had forgotten something vital like waxed paper to preserve leaves or an empty jar for insects.

"It's alright, I've got some extra" (peanut-butter jars), "and we can share."

"We're ready," came the cry in unison, as if they were attempting the north slope of Everest. They fell into some sort of order behind Morgan.

The day was of spun gold and blue. They marched through mown fields and pastures. The belled cow shook her head to clang a warning; it was all but ignored. The other cows lifted their heads curiously, but never stopped chewing. They had been turned out into the harvested fields to clean them up. They grazed like giants on the stubble.

Clouds of dust rose behind the children. They sang rounds in the valley but saved their breath as they began to climb into the forest. Morgan felt so much more real among these children, who recognized him, reacted to him, allowed him his being. They shouted and interrupted when spoken to, were exuberant, joyful, delighted with themselves. When they were hurt it was excruciating; they wept until their faces turned purple. All the shocks and surprises of the out-side showed on their impetuous skins.

That day children were lost and found. Together they held a small funeral for a dead bird, buried it and fashioned a small stick cross. They were naughty. They stole each other's sandwiches. "I only borrowed it," said Tommy, smacking his lips after a slice of ham. A mayonnaise jar broke and gave Carla a nasty cut. "Put moss on it to draw out the poison, that's what the Indians do." Billy slid head-first down the whole side of a hill and swallowed "at least a ton of dirt!" Jill got so excited over an acorn find that she was sick and the mess had to be covered over with leaves.

87

Sally ran into a bush (thank God it was not a tree) when the boys chased her with a wriggling vine. The children came and went, tugged on Morgan's coat to show him a tiny fistful, a bug who did not survive the ordeal, but was filed away in the bottom of a pocket for later identification and dissection. The whole day was as natural as a lifetime.

On the way back everyone was tired and grubby. They put their gathered treasures on their desks, the jars only after Morgan had punched breathing holes with an ice pick in the tin tops. Then they were all gone. Morgan sat alone on the platform, chin in hands. The little wind left in the late afternoon blew the children's leaves on the desks. He got up and closed the door. His face felt burned from the fresh air. The day had been successful.

In the middle of the golden flush of days, the tail of a hurricane spun crazily toward the coast. It was Morgan who first heard the warnings on his radio and ran down to the village. Boats were drawn up, lashed in a spider-web of ropes or anchored in the middle of the harbour in hopes they could ride it out. Shutters were closed on front windows. Paraphernalia was gathered from littered yards and brought inside. Loose cows, goats, chickens were herded inside barns and the doors were fastened. Dogs were called in or allowed to crawl under the houses. The air lay like a wet towel. When everything was gathered in there was nothing to do but wait and that was the most difficult. The storm might by-pass them entirely; on the other hand tales were still told about the hurricane nine years ago that tore off roofs, battered boats and ruined the unharvested fields.

Morgan and Sibbi sat in the stone house on the hill that had withstood all winds. There was the peculiar tension and pressure of calm.

"This is what it's like in your head, isn't it Sibbi, this deadly grey, the weight of silence, the endless waiting until it just gets lost in forever? I think sometimes you must be very strong, to be so lost."

But she was making no conscious comparisons. Her sphere was often as uncluttered by time and strife as a dreamless sleep. She was inattentive. Morgan touched her. Her skin was as warm as his own. Surprised, he took her wrist; her pulse was steady, slower than his, for she felt as much anticipation as a stone. The pressure was too much for him; he got up and paced back and forth, then stopped, hardly breathing.

The sky thickened and sank on the land. The waves on the shore, pulled by opposite poles of energy, didn't unroll, but heaved up and down without showing white water. Every animal swallowed its own voice. There was nothing to take its place. Leaves hung like dogs' ears. Birds sat in their bushes waiting, looking all round for what they did not know, their wings held firmly to their sides.

Morgan decided to check all the windows and shutters. He put a huge log onto the fire. Then he got his boots out of the cupboard, his raincoat and hat off the wall. He got the same things for Sibbi. They looked like slippery black prehistoric reptiles. Morgan took the precaution of tying a length of soft rope around Sibbi's waist so he could hold onto her.

It was nearly dark outside. Morgan let the latch clatter shut in its socket. It was the loudest sound. They stood at the gate in the back yard.

Suddenly an isolated clump of bush by the fence began to shiver. There were spaces in the air as it began to rain. Then heavily. Still there was no wind. Morgan took Sibbi around to the front of the house, along the path, which was already glistening. There was no light left in the sky. If he hadn't taken these steps to the stone wall a hundred thousand times they could have been lost. Behind, between the black gusts of rain, he could see the faint glow of firelight in the slits between the shutters. The great horn sounded from the gut of the lighthouse. They stood at the wall, separate, each holding onto the stones, Morgan with a piece of rope in his hand.

Then into the night came the sound of the wind, beginning like a gasp released out of a pit in the ground, from under a wave or through a hole in the ink-black sky. As a speck of dust gathers vapour to make a raindrop, this insubstantial wind hurried over the sea and hurled itself onto the land. The very roots of the trees shuddered. Underground streams faltered. The great backs of the hills groaned. The sea rose out of its bed. Like a million lashing sails, the waves tore off, were flung into the air and smashed into the cliffs. Flanks of streaming water poured over the rocks, withdrew and surged again and again. There was no light but the white waves; there was no sound but the wind. Nor did it seem there ever had been or would be again.

It invaded Sibbi's lungs. She hung on in shock, her mouth gaping open, swallowing the wind. The rain bit her face, flew into her eyes. She opened her eyes wider and wider, for the grey was gone, replaced by the black storm and nothing else.

A broken bird swept by, its useless wings wide open, then was gone. The earth was twisted, then everything swung in a circle, a pulsing vortex. Marooned colours appeared in the swells and were consumed by the wind.

Morgan listened for lulls in the storm. He wanted to get back inside the house. The short path was too long, the wind too strong; they would be blown away. He was drenched through; rain streamed down his face, even his ears were full of water. He was angry for having been so foolish as to go out, and he was afraid. This was inhuman. He pulled Sibbi down on the ground. They would have to crawl back under the protection of the wall. Anything, any way to reach home safely. It was a shock to Morgan to feel the chill of physical fear. Fear for his skin and bones. They crawled along the muddy trench, he tugged and Sibbi came along behind, gasping. Her weight; the mud, cold and moving; the stone wall straining in the wind, wet and dark. The rocks remembering their birth in cold caves. His hands sank in the mud.

When they reached the wood fence and had crawled through, he stood up, put his arm around Sibbi's waist and hung onto the rail with his other arm. The wind screamed. It came from all directions at once. He staggered on the beaten grass. It wasn't much farther, but he was exhausted. Later he would be able to think all kinds of thoughts about primitive man and awe. The gods of wind and weather would find a blood-brother in Morgan. Now all he wanted was to get to the door, open it and collapse inside, in safety.

For a few moments, once they were inside and the door shut, Morgan stood still. The wind and rain beat on the house and drove the fire in the chimney, but didn't touch them anymore. A flush of relief as deep as his heart warmed Morgan. He stripped off his heavy wet clothing, left it in a heap on the floor and put on a dressing-gown. Sibbi stood gulping like a fish. He undid the rope around her waist and took off the slicker. Only the top of her head under her hat was dry. He rubbed her down with a towel, marveling that her thin bones were still whole. He wrapped her in a quilt and sat her in front of the fire. She was shivering, her teeth chattering up and down on each other. Morgan was momentarily glad she was still mute; she wouldn't tell tales of his foolishness.

He made tea for them and sorted out the steaming pile of clothing, hanging pieces near the fire and in the pantry. He rebuilt the fire, lifted the inert Sibbi and put her to bed under the clattering shutters, tucking her in tightly. Her eyes were already closed, but her breathing was governed by the storm. Morgan went to his room and collapsed into bed. He had trouble sleeping, though he wasn't sure whether the violence was outside or inside his head.

What was left in the limpid cool morning was a shattered land. Morgan opened the shutters, the windows and the door. The air was sweet, gentle. It moved about hesitantly. It was new, coming out of the soft faded mist, which lay folded in the hollows, on the tide-flows. The trees were still, their sides stretched raw, wet dark branches down in the mud, some snapped in two. White stumps like splintered glass oozed in the weak watery sun. Leaves hung limp, as still as before the storm only now they were on the other side; they had survived.

Morgan left Sibbi asleep and went into the village to see what had happened there. He shared a secret with the earth that he wasn't sure he wanted. He didn't know what to do with this new experience. Almost everything he had learned before had a purpose, practical or intellectual. Here was an immaculate knowledge, an awe that had involved bone, blood and brain. Yet when he consciously called upon his brain, the knowing evaporated into the translucent sky. When he felt his bone it went dumb as a stone. And his blood was as undecipherable as an ancient hieroglyph.

But when he abandoned his footsteps to the green-white morning this trinity soared. The bitter and the sweet, two wings, beat together triumphant in the arch of sky.

Wraiths of mist were flowing out into the harbour, re-vealing eroded gutters, smashed flowerbeds; then trailing out on the glass-quiet water, where the waves lapped like tongues from under its surface onto the ragged shore, floated the boats. Men were rowing out to inspect for damage they hoped was non-existent. Women rested their elbows on porch railings or leaned on brooms that were clogged with leaves and mud. The sun was stronger now and cast sha-dows of children, out in cotton and gum-boots.

Except for rivers of mud, a few shingles up-ended and shed doors blown from their hinges, all was well.

A woman stopped him. "It's just a miracle we weren't blown down last night. I swear I never heard such wind coming on nine years now—not since the last storm when Jenkins lost his boat and shed and we found him under it in the morning hiding in the salt box; came up all white as a sheet he did, and this time no boats lost and only Jacob's dog, poor thing, always was spooky in the weathers. . . . It's curious isn't it Mr. Morgan. . . . What makes a hurricane?"

He was surprised at her question. She shifted onto her other hip while he gave a text-book explanation. In the end she was most impressed by the fact that they were "foreign."

When he was assured that life would go on despite all the tales, Morgan went home to clean up his own back yard. Sibbi had wakened first ahead of a nightmare and wasn't yet sure what being awake had in store for her. She clung nervously to the table when Morgan came in. He started to fix himself large sandwiches of cheese and meat, growing ravenous as the air freshened. It was poignant that his new-found sensibility had to be so private. He who was a teacher, an imparter of knowledge and experience, was burdened with a secret.

"Oh, Sibbi, Sibbi," he said sadly.

"What?"

"Sibbi?"

"What is it? What's the matter?" Her voice held real concern; her eyes were bright and direct.

Before Morgan could speak again she was hurled into the nightmare. It seized her bodily and shook her with a force greater than any hurricane. Morgan dropped the knife and caught her as she reeled into the pit. Sweat seethed out of her skin. She turned ice-blue. Her breath hissed when it struck the hot air.

"Sibbi, no, no, you're not going to be punished for coming out," he shouted as he kneeled astride her, holding her arms to the floor beside her head so she wouldn't hurt it.

"D'you hear me? Listen to me!" Holding her took a great effort. "I've got you by the tail, you're not going to keep falling into the pit, you're not getting to the bottom this time, because I've got hold of you, damn it, can't you feel it. . . ?" Her tortured face worked back and forth, her eyes open but seeing nothing, wandered back and forth out of rhythm with the rest of her. She made Morgan seasick so he lowered his head, not looking at her.

When she finally stopped and he felt her knees at his back as she tried to roll up, he got off her and let her coil into a foetal shape.

When Morgan caught his breath he was hungrier than before. He ate his sandwiches and pulled himself together once again. Her voice had been deeper than he had imagined. It wasn't a child's voice; too husky for her small body. It was unnerving, the way she spoke; so organized. It was as if she had invaded his thoughts and questioned his anxiety rather than the other way round. He wanted her secrets, her private being opened to him, but she had found his first. And at terrible cost. He was angry at her for answering. The very yearning he had been looking for all morning. Perhaps she was saying she knew something about the feelings the hurricane had evoked in him; perhaps that she knew how he felt; or perhaps she was simply responding to his tone, one she hadn't heard before. Perhaps she'd just heard him for the first time.

All afternoon while Morgan straightened fence-posts, raked debris and threw branches out into the woods he thought about the impossibility of defining another person.

8

It was more difficult to come out each succeeding spring. Through the years Sibbi's no-man's-land up in the hills spread its borders and developed a landscape of its own. Of gullies, rifts, seams. Dry rocks glistened with her perspiration and became treacherous. Jason had chosen to be separate; Sibbi could do nothing else.

She hung on. To survive she had found places inside herself where she could go. And when Jason worked at home she went into the meadows with the white sheep and the dog. When he took the sheep out, she remained in the garden, killing slugs in a can of turpentine, pulling weeds, stirring the earth.

They were together at breakfast, supper and at night, all in a twilight of silence. They were together when the ewes were yeaning, when the lambs were castrated and their tails docked; during the shearing, and midsummer, when the sheep were washed in the rain-softened streams. Those times Jason needed her and she loved it. Even though memory taunted her like the moon at noon and, remembering, pinched her heart.

Jason had built a little pen on one side of the stream and herded all the sheep into it. One by one they were taken out and led into the deep swift water that washed burrs, mites and stains out of their thick winter coats. When they were led out the other side bleating, they were quite often too heavy to stand on their own. Water poured off them as it does off polar bears coming up on the ice. Jason's strong hands did not tire, squeezing out the water. When the sheep stopped streaming like waterfalls and could walk, they were released into the hot dry wind.

"Hold 'em steady now," Jason commanded. Sibbi shone to a blind eye. But when it was all over and they were drenched, the sheep gorgeous, fluffed and bleached white, they stood together and actually laughed at each other's bedraggled appearance.

The sheep grazed like fallen clouds in an inverted sky.

Shortly after they were shorn they alternately frolicked,

free of the weight of wool or shivered, embarrassed in their wrinkled skins.

Jason tied the loose wool blankets into bales, put them in the cart and went to the village. One summer, he returned with a sturdy tiger-dun pony. Its expression was careful and resigned; dark eyes with brown circles around them. Brown rimmed his ears, peppered his plume-like mane and ran a stripe down the middle of his back into his tail. He had motley brown-pearl hooves and brown stockings. Jason put hobbles on his front legs and let him graze with the sheep. He had built another pen one spring and brought back a pig with coarse white hair and pink undersides, which he would slaughter before snowfall. And a crate of cackling hens who could live on a special roost in the hay shed. Sibbi had to get to know the hens before she could reach under their soft bellies to steal their eggs. The pig had been nearly grown; besides she hadn't wanted to become attached to it. But the pony was different.

"Can I ride him?" she asked, offering a carrot and tops on a flat palm.

"Yes, I suppose so." He made a spliced rope hackamore, put Sibbi up on the round spineless back and gave her a riding lesson. A new world offered itself. The pony's legs went *swish swish* through the swampy grass. He set his feet down soundlessly on the dust and pine-needle carpet of the hilltops. The pony wasn't as busy as the dog and could be her companion. They'd gone far into the green and bidding land where the sun was whole and the blue-green wood primeval. They'd stopped for a picnic in a milky way of flowers.

On the way back Sibbi lay on the pony's back, her head on the soft padded rump. She was floating above the ground, the earth known only through the hinge of the pony's body. The sun freckled oriental patterns through the surface of the trees. A lid of leaves intercepted the light. Sibbi was warm and unborn. Spaces of peace spread inside her, un-assaulted by bleak hopes shot through with undefined demands. In a green shade of simply being she was folded like a bud, waiting out a spring frost. Dusky the trunks marched by the corner of her eye. They thrust up, fragmented into branches, shattered into thousands of flirting leaves, turning. The pony's head lobbed back and forth, snorting with its velvet brown nose, twin jets in the brown dust. The pony didn't trifle with the sky, even one as bland-blue as this. She could ride through all of summer this way.

For Jason the shape of everything had become deadly serious. Sibbi watched his hands holding a knife-blade against the grinding stone. He tested the steel, the razor-sharp edge proof of his competence, his cautious finger touching it. Jason didn't trifle with sheep, steel, storm, the night-owl or the fragile violet. Sibbi saw how he watched what he did with his hands, but she couldn't see what he watched in his own soul. Bears stood in his eyes. His rigid skin did not absorb the sound of the loon. Jason made white noise, toneless vibrations like a waterfall.

When she was a little older, she would realize: "No-one is extra bad to me or extra good; I'm just ignored."Each fall by the end of September the year's growing had ceased. Only the ripening was left. Sibbi began to gather in. Crows gave her withering looks when she climbed into the fruit trees and stole their crop. She dug potatoes from under shriven plants, carrots, beets, turnips, onions; pulled cucumbers out of the manure and beans out of the hopeless tangle of vines. She worked in still-warm days where the only sound was the faint echo left in the hole after she had pulled a vegetable out of the ground and the solid thud as she threw them into piles. Sometimes the pig grunted for roots; she gave it wormy ones. The crows, like vultures, watched; shoulders hunched above their backs: blue-black blades.

In the scrub land she gathered vivid bunchberries, black-berries and blue-grey juniper berries. Green acorns pebbled the forest. She took a basket home to the pig. The trees began to wear yellow and red leaves like trinkets.

At night the sheep smelled the ice coming down over the tree-tops and bunched together. In the morning, night-shaken leaves were sprinkled in the low green grass. The sun rode steadily south over the earth. Some days the sky was glacial.

The things of the earth no longer seemed careful of themselves the way they had in the first impulse of spring.

Now the skins of summer were being shed. Leaves lost their green autonomy and became the gold-red of the sun. Finally possessed, they would become the brown dust of the earth.

Red leaves were drops of blood on the ground. Maple leaves like the devil's fork abandoned before ice.

The harvest was gathered in on top of leaf fall. Jason pulled up a floorboard and the root crops were laid in cold sand. Sibbi put the board back in place and the corner seemed warm because of the captured season of grown things. She felt safer with the cache under the floor boards.

Then there was time to be idle; the ewes wouldn't be bred until December. She rode the pony skilfully now, out into the shining land, the burnished dying land. For a while. For a while she rode through the golden peace. She left the cabin slowly, but the speed increased. She clung to the pony's sides with her knees and urged him to a canter. His tail blew out behind him; Sibbi's hair blew away behind her face. The sky hurt, it was so blue and enormous. When they stopped and there was no wind, she fed the pony an apple and ate one herself. She picked long-stemmed clover and wove a garland, a halo of purple to set on her head. Another for the pony's forelock, only he shook his head until it fell out and he ate it.

She was alone, no-one was leaning over her. She took the rope reins and led the pony up a forest hill. They kept their heads down. It was warm and dry. Air barely moved in the branches. Under the trees was a thick layer of pine needles, their smell thick and dusty. The pony sneezed. At the top of the hill there was a clear space with weather-beaten grass cropped between the flaking rocks. Sun and wind. To the east she saw the ocean and a mountainous bank of fog waiting for dusk. To the west the land lay in the sun, green and brown. And bare, except right below her in the first valley. There were three caravans, their canvas tops like burned earth. And three sleek burnished horses tethered in separate circles.

It was the gypsy camp. Other outsiders, others remote. Sibbi watched the quietly grazing horses until some women came out of the wagons, meeting around a fire she hadn't seen for the sun. Their long full skirts mushroomed like umbrellas when they crouched at the fire. Their shawls were irridescent. Black, blue and red silk stung through with gold, green and silver threads. The material shone like night rainbows, brighter than the fire. When the wind fell softly away the voices of the women came up the hill.

She wanted to go down the hill and belong for a while. But these were gypsies. She was frightened and clutched at the pony so as not to be stolen or bewitched. As quickly as she could she retreated down the hill, led the pony to a stump and prepared to mount. He sidestepped nervously and she coaxed and pulled until his back was beside the stump. She didn't notice when the gypsy boy came up the path and stopped.

"Hello" he said and brushed his thick hair aside. His face was in full sunshine; it disappeared. The sun froze on it.

Sibbi started; the pony shied and she was left standing like King of the Mountain on the stump, alone. Sound glimmered and sank into her ears. The crown of clover pricked her skin. Her hands, empty.

Still she didn't speak. He couldn't see her eyes under a sheaf of straw hair. He pulled his hand out of his pocket and went after the pony who was munching quietly on a hummock of sweet dry grass. The pony showed no surprise at his touch and followed him back to her. The boy stood in the shadow of the dark side of the mountain and could see her.

And she him. Finally coming out of herself, she moved into the eclipse of his eyes, his rainbow of skin—for a good deal of his skin was showing here and there. Feet naked and half his legs; his hands blatantly bare, one holding the rope, the other over the pony's withers. In the autumn chill, he wore a sleeveless shirt. His skin was darker than dirty mud. His eyes were facts. Not gentle, unassuming or dreamy like the teacher's in school. Not hard as the permafrost in Jason's eyes. These, coal-black, showed the sunshine stuff they were made of. Ages captured in his eyes, not conquered by candle-lit literature or put to death by discipline. Sibbi felt his eyes on her like a hawk. He saw absolutely everything twitching on the earth. Like a house covered with ivy, he was aware of the wind.

And he knew something she didn't. He slouched there, inside her silence, a place he seemed to have discovered. She felt invaded but didn't know where; there was nothing she could do. She felt uncomfortable, unwhole.

"D'you want your pony?" he said and held the rope toward her. She took it and the wind came around a corner. It wove around her until she was marooned. He pushed the pony to her. Its back was sun-warm. As she mounted she looked at the top of his head; the swirl of crow-black hair —a whirlpool of sea sucking all the ships and sailors into its centre, and the sun. Then there was nothing else to do but ride away.

Once the surprise was over and she was in the deep woods

on the path toward home, she remembered and was rather lonely.

Later in the night when the cold tucked its feathers and flew into valleys, she lay under the rough blankets and remembered. The meeting had been in a no-man's-land. No props, no belongings, no place to hide. She opened her eyes wider and wider as the fire settled in its ashes and darkness opened its hand. She looked boldly at the gypsy boy, who was still looking at her.

In a month the days were white and mysterious. Sibbi slipped out under the cover of frosty fog to go to the school. To hear human voices since Jason hadn't spoken for a while. At her desk, hunched against the cold, she kept adjusting her hair on her shoulders, touching fingers to her lips. One grown man and many children in the schoolroom. And herself. Nowhere. Now, feeling herself separate. Nowhere.

School ended in the curfew of dusk. Sibbi regained enough presence to get out the door first, to escape the rest of the children. Tonight they all just wanted to go home. Halfway up the bluff Sibbi stopped. Nearly everything was invisible. Wraiths of ice-cold mist streamed around her feet. Here on these idle slopes she had spent most of her conscious life. And in this icy fog. Something drifted like vapour between her and the village, between her and the school, between her and Jason. Externally these places and beings, an opaque skin holding her life together. Inside was a tangle of roots, pushing this way and that, blind thriving roots. She pulled her sweater double over her chest, then crossed her arms and hunched her shoulders to protect her neck. The only light in the whole world came from the school. Diffused in the clouds, it stained them yellow. Other lights were swallowed in the thick cold dusk. Sibbi was shivering so hard she ran up the hill in a fast, jerking stride.

The cabin was empty. The furniture stood in a dark vault, lifeless, angular, the table bare, the chest closed like a dead log, the bed drowned in a damp green rug. She rummaged in the mouldy ashes to find a live spark but there was none. So she started from scratch, built a fire of papers and kindling. She lit a candle and put it on the table. Finally the fire hissed and drew, giving her wonderful heat and light. She stood before it until she could unwrap her sweater, then filled the iron pot with water and swung it over the flames.

Where was Jason in this dusk? She didn't want him to be there, she wanted to know where he was. She didn't want him to sneak up on her.

When she was thoroughly warm and dry, when the boiled dinner was bubbling in the pot, she put a sheepskin on her shoulders and peered outside. It was black. She could taste salt in the fog and feel it in her eyes. The animals stirred when the light sprang in the lantern. She checked the pony and the pig in the lean-to. The chickens were offended and snapped open their yellow bills. Only the sheep didn't move, weighted down perhaps by the mist in their wool. Everyone was accounted for except Jason. Sibbi returned uneasily to the cabin. She hung the lantern on a hook under the eave by the door, left it lit like a beacon.

Inside she sat down on the bench, then got up, returning moments later with a half-loaf of bread and butter. She sat again and broke off bits of the bread, swabbed them in the butter and put them in her mouth. An uneasy truce was in the cabin. The peace of a crackling fire and water brewing, the solemnity of wood all round. But there was that void; a black hole in which the silent shape of Jason belonged. It had come to this. He occupied space like a stone and, when he wasn't there, the hole showed.

She didn't know what time it was. She put more logs on the fire. Supper was cooked. She pulled the pot away from the direct flame and spooned some into a bowl. She sat again, holding her face above the steam. The candle-wick tumbled into a puddle of wax on the table and went out.

While her stew cooled, she poked at the tendrils of wax with her nail. The shadows in the room were harsher now; her own shadow stooped over her, following the curve of the ceiling. Bending her head back she saw it and was frightened.

She fancied things. Something was misplaced in the night. Mists settled in the hollows of the land like snow, without a sound. All the noise was inside the cabin; there was nothing from outside. She ate, put yet another log on the crackling fire, then fell asleep at the table, beneath her arm, beneath her shadow.

The mist froze on the splintery grass, frosted the naked withdrawn trees. It touched everything. There was no sound or smell or sight, except the small halo of yellow kerosene burning in the gloom.

Then the dog barked, the latch sprang open and all kinds of people were stumbling into her dreams. Standing, holding onto the edge of the table, she saw Jason being carried into the cabin. He was laid on the bed, overcome with huge shadows. Sibbi swivelled round to watch; a voice told her to light lanterns and hang them above the bed so they could see. After this was done she looked up into the semi-circle of faces around Jason. It wasn't the townsfolk, it was the gypsies, wrapped against the cold, dark bare heads bent over the still form on the bed. She looked from one to another, then to Jason. Someone's hands were opening his clothing, asking for water and a cloth, for there was blood and it had glued his clothes to his skin. The shadows and the blood, she couldn't see clearly. Jason wasn't moving, but he seemed to be quivering in the flame.

The boy from the hollow woods was there with three other men and a curious child who still clutched the rope that had been put on the dog. Sibbi knelt. The dog was under the bed, safe from feet. She loosened the rope from his neck, and looked into his shiny wet eyes. Jason groaned. She stood up and the men began talking over him while they washed him and took off his clothes. She heard little; nothing stuck in her brain. Someone handed her a bowl of blood, mud and water. After staring at it for a moment, she carried it outside to empty it, then filled it with fresh warm water. A man took it and set it next to Jason on the bed. His clothes were nearly all cut away; a shredded heap on the floor. Yet he didn't make another sound. The men touched his arms and legs, then pressed their fingers to his collarbones, ribs, hip bones. Nothing was broken. With his clothes gone he was so white and the oozing wounds stood out like branches against the moon. Why didn't he move? The whites of his eyes had a dead look when one man lifted the lids.

The room was unbearably hot and smelled like a swamp. Sibbi turned away. One hand held the table; the other, cold and dry, pressed to her forehead. Nothing was clear save the hard marks on Jason's skin. The gypsy boy came up behind her, caught her across the back and led her outside. He clicked the latch behind them. She shivered though her skin burned. She reached toward the still lantern but the boy took her arm.

"Can you talk?" he asked.

She found his face, the words, then remembered she hadn't spoken under the hill.

"Yes," she nodded.

"We found him after he fell down a hill. Was cutting wood or marking 'em for later and the axe musta jumped outa his hand, knocking him out on the forehead. He's lain a good while 'afore we come 'long, that's why the blood's so old on him. We've not found a thing serious if he's a-right in the head and comes to. . . ."

"Thank you," said Sibbi. It was the first time in years she'd said that, or anything. It was difficult to know what else to say.

"Do you know what to do?"

"Do?"

"To keep him warm an' make sure the blood don't start again, an' don't let him thrash about, not knowing...."

"Yes," she said.

The boy cupped his large hand under her chin, lifted it so he could see her face. It was very soft by lamplight and wet with mist. "I'll come by tomorrow if you like, to see how he is."

She hummed. He put her chin down and opened the door. The men were finished. Jason lay clean and covered, only his head and neck out from under the quilt that Sibbi had made. The little boy hung onto the bed, his cheek down on his arm. The men helped themselves to some bread and they all used the same mug to drink a cup of stew broth.

The eldest man wiped his mouth on his sleeve and said, "If you've Comfrey or Healing Herb, boil some up to lay on the wounds, helps 'em to green up and some of this 'ere broth'll do fine...." He stared at the girl for a moment silently. "I'd get the town doctor tomorrow, miss," thinking, she's got a queer sort of face, unused to being seen.

Then everyone was gone. The hole filled up with silence. The logs settled and struck out a glitter of sparks. She filled the fireplace to keep the room warm. Once she was up she brought in several logs from the pile at the side of the cabin, so they could dry. She sat at the table, but got up every few minutes to lean over the bed, her hands fluttering around the edge of the quilt. Never quite touching it. She bent over, putting her ear over his breath, listening above the fire. She washed her own face several times and walked around the cabin. One time when she sat at the table she fell asleep suddenly. The mists twitched as cat's tails do when they sleep. The night was no different though, for all the fierce drama in it.

And when the dawn rose over the hills with a fresh cold wind, the animals broke out of their night huddles. The dog woke up in his place under the bed, stretched and was hungry. No-one had fed him yesterday. He climbed up on the table and ate the hunk of bread. Then licked the butter plate clean. Jumping down he found half a bucket of water. He went to the window, stood up on his hind legs and sniffed the sill. Then to the door, running his nose along its edges. It was time he was to his sheep. Finally the whine in his throat broke.

Sibbi rolled her head up onto her arm. Her eyes opened on the raw wood of the table. She was stiff and shivered in the morning light. The blanket she pulled around her shoulders did no good. She let the dog out the door, then built up the fire. Before attempting to look at the bed and its burden, she went to the window. Outside grey, but bush and evergreen branch were giving way to the wind. The wind would blow all day from the northwest, blueing the sky, turning down the last cover on the land, preparing for snow.

When she had looked at the day, she walked over to Jason. She could hear him breathing. The quilt rose and fell steadily on his chest. In the light, she could touch him, barely. The back of her hand to his cool forehead, her fingers on the raw sticky weal that ran across his chest. The wound was hot. When she touched it again, he moved in pain, waking. The ceiling and walls were straight and solid in the day. He saw Sibbi too, pale, as if she belonged back in night.

"Oh, you'll live then," she whispered to herself.

Jason cringed to think death had been that close to him. He looked up and remembered the second he hadn't paid attention to the axe; the axe ringing on a hardwood knot, bouncing back at him. . . .

"How. . . how did you find me?"

"Didn't. Some men brought you home after dark."

"Some men?"

"Yes."

106

"Am I. . . what's happened to me?" It scalded him to ask.

"If you woke up, they said. Nothing broke, only he has to wake up. . ."

"Yes?"

"They said I might go for the doctor today."

"No."

Of course, she'd known he would say that. Maybe she should just go, but she wasn't sure how to walk away from Jason.

"What should I do while you're down?"

"Some water."

Not only a cup of water, but some new bread and a bowl of broth set nearby. He could drink by himself when she put a log under the pillow.

A simple schedule: the animals, feeding and watering them. The woodpile replenished, the gates and fences looked at—that was all. Sibbi pulled on winter clothes and went out.

Jason dozed and woke again. He couldn't stay asleep long enough. He didn't want to lie there and have to think in the silence that hovered under the ceiling. Who had touched him? Who had found him in the woods and brought him home? Who had washed the wounds the forest had cut into his skin? His sister probably wouldn't know their names; she'd never met anyone in town. And who from town was on business in the deep woods? His head was tired, his limbs lay in the hollows they had made in the mattress. He slept again. And woke briefly to the sound of the latch opening, then closing. Sibbi moving in the cabin.

"Done," she reported. "Everything's done for the day." Darkness slipped across the land silently and brought snow that night. Sibbi made up a bed for herself on the floor halfway between Jason and the warm hearth stones. She persuaded the dog to lie against her and put her hand on his neck for warmth. Just before she fell asleep she remembered that the gypsy boy hadn't come that day as he'd said he would.

Again the dog woke her. Stiff and cold, the fire crumpled into a remnant of coals; but she had at least slept a full night through. She hurried the fire and went to Jason. His nose was cold, but the rest of him was alive. He woke up when the cabin was warm. As he ate porridge and broth, he asked her who it was had carried him back.

"I don't know," she lied.

Jason finished and fell back into sleep. She banked the fire, put on the sheepskin and went outside. The hill lay breathless, blindingly white: the white backs of sheep in the brand-new snow. No wind had come to brush it from the fence-tops and trees. Everything was touched. Shadows that came over the morning hill were thin, diffused, and the sun was orange. She was heavy and alone. She didn't like Jason to have to depend on her. She might betray him. In ignorance. Jason had told her often that they were alone, that she should be glad of him. Of that time before she only remembered moods: of a great gold dome of sky and the smell of hay, of a woman who was plump and warm, of a woman made of thorns and ribbons. . . .

The dog dove into a snowdrift. He came out with overhanging eyebrows of snow and a heap on his nose. A smile stretched across Sibbi's face, a moment of peace melted through her. It was to be a fine crisp day.

In the dim shed she gathered a basket of eggs from the warm chicken nests. From the high stack of bales she tumbled one down to drag out to the sheep. The sunlight pierced her from all sides and below. The sheep moved in, crowding as she cut the bale loose. They lost some of their smell in the cold.

Carefully she took the small hatchet and chopped a hole in the ice that grew over the stream. It was while she was ladling water into the bucket with the scoop that the gypsy boy called to her through the slanted shadows. Sibbi pulled down the visor on her cap. The glare was still strong.

"Hello. Are you all better inside there?"

He came as close to her as he had been the other night under the lantern.

"He's not up."

"But he's not dead."

She breathed in. "No."

He reached up and brushed some snow from her cap.

"Well that's good; what can I do?"

"I. . . I've done it all here."

He looked around, catching the sheep at the last of the hay, the dog standing pensively, even the basket of white eggs in the snow by the shed door.

"Or anything inside?"

"Oh, no." She surprised herself.

He looked into her head again.

"I mean he doesn't know who it was saved him and I don't think he'd like to know it was you. He doesn't like other people who live apart, like we do. . . ."

The boy stood quietly where he was, then took the ladle and filled the bucket. He carried it to the cabin for her, but on the way he leaned against the weight and asked, "Is he fair to you?"

Sibbi didn't know what to answer.

"You're not used to people, are you?"

"No." Only this time she wasn't frightened.

In winter the sun was so far south in the sky that it never reached this side of the cabin. They stood in shadow that was brown and warm. The boy put the bucket on the step and looked out at the rude farm. Sibbi was very close to him. She studied the thin white line around his head between his browned skin and black hair. The edges of his ear were red. He had a man's bones already grown in his face; his skin hadn't caught up.

When he turned to her and smiled, she smiled back.

"And you're sure you don't want me to look at him?"

"No."

"Well, I'm off then," and he walked out into the bright yard. Sibbi stood only a moment before running after him.

"Wait," she called, when out of hearing from the cabin; "wait," she said to his face. They stood a few feet apart. "Will you come back again?"

"To see you."

"Yes." And she wasn't shy.

The boy shaded his eyes. She was so terribly fair. The morning sun streamed through her; her hair was like a net cast before the light. But mostly he was caught by the blue that seemed to lie beneath the surface of her skin. The same blue that hides in ice, that comes from the sea of the sky. She was alone, transparent. For an instant he saw this.

"I'll come again." He saw her slim, young and fair.

Sibbi watched him walk around the sheep pen, down through the drifted valley to the edge of the woods. She watched past the sound of his going, then stared again at the silver-black trunks of trees.

At noon the snow began to melt. The next day it was all gone and the sheep were on the grass again.

The boy didn't come that day or the next. Or the several days following. Jason rode out his fevers and his wounds sealed up with red scars. His hand hung out over the side of the bed and he drummed his fingers on the wood, over and over. Sibbi washed her hair and sat before the fire to brush it dry. She was stronger now, had done all manner of things by herself and knew someone, a place she would rather be sometimes. She hadn't thought before, this place or that place, she was just where she happened to be. She thought about the caravans under the hill; women's talk and laughter bright in the air. The shawls knotted across their bosoms. And the boy living his life. Other people had always been bstract for her, everyone, even Jason, though she knew nore about him than he imagined. But he didn't want to be known, and didn't admit her. Now she had actually poken to someone; he had looked at her and seen part of her she didn't know existed. As the teacher had invited her vith words, this boy tantalized her with his eyes. She was varm and restless. This was something different from the low mellow season the schoolroom offered; this was a pringing curiosity, impatient in the winter way of her life.

The tide of the sun fell back. Jason walked outside in the un and continued to heal. More hay was brought. He went o town for supplies with his cap pulled down to his eyebrows.

When the sun showed only thin white foam in the southern sky the ewes were bred to the ram.

Sibbi did as much as she could inside the cabin to keep busy, to prevent the shadows that came with the fire. She went to school on Christmas Day, for the days were no different to her. The building was empty and stone cold, but she went in and walked around the mute, worn benches. Her body was so direct, her blood speaking so loud even here that she couldn't hear the voice of the teacher. Her skin was too tight to feel his gentleness. She felt a loss.

And in the banked hills and woods, in the slow smoke of a sky preparing to snow, she felt a longing.

In the cabin she felt overdue. Instead of being still, she wanted to move. She was restless and ungiving. But because she was small it wasn't noticed by Jason; things she did were done stealthily, silently. Half the time she wasn't there. As Jason had his private plans, so had she withdrawn into herself. At night, she got into bed as soon as possible, next to the wall, under the window. She puffed up the pillow, leaned back into it, pulling her knees up under the blankets and quilt. The flame was broken up in the window but she could see out into the goblin-dark night when she leaned her head just so, hiding the lamp. It was in that curious dark country she hid her thoughts.

Everything was still. Even the moon seemed frozen, a thin scythe. The animals were sluggish; the trees slept above ground; the bush was brittle and grey; earth and stone were as one. Even Jason moved more slowly, more methodically. Snow was a burden. Drifts buried sections of the fence which he had to clear. The water trough had to be filled while the sheep were penned and bales of hay broken open for them to eat. He had to go back into the woods to cut trees for next winter's firewood.

Sibbi had boots that winter, which gave her greater freedom. One afternoon she put them on and walked down the bluff toward the point. The white sky as bland as milk. On the hill, the snow muffled all sound. It had been blown into folds, gathered beneath ledges. She wrapped her scarf across her nose and scuffed underneath the snow to the edge of the cliff. There the salt wind struck her; it threw the sea above the high-tide lines, where it froze. Pieces of grotesque ice, scarred by the salt, heavier than the stone beneath. Where ground juniper grew the ice had licked the branches, made patterns like frost on window-glass. Beyond, the great blue ocean boiled, white water blown from the peaks of swells, blown like clouds above the sky.

It was there, at land's end, in the pressing cold that the gypsy boy called to her. Led her through the pink-grey dusk to his silk black horse tied among dark evergreens. It was darker in the trees and she couldn't see what colour the shawl was that he put over her head and shoulders. She pressed a bit of it to her cheek and smelt purple lavender. The boy helped her onto the horse, then got on behind her, reaching around to hold the reins. There was no hurry; time had suddenly become an apparition, moving through spaces hitherto unoccupied. Sibbi leaned back against his chest, letting his arms come around her. No-one had touched her ince she was six years old.

He let her wear the beautiful silk-thread shawl. He let her
ide his great black horse through the snow on the hills.
And he let her go into his caravan to be warmed. It was
haped like a loaf, a cave. Moulded around bentwood staves,
he tarred canvas was stretched taut and laced down. It was
quite waterproof; snow slipped off. Inside it was warm with
eds and raw wood. There were richly patterned materials
lung on the walls to keep in the warmth. A small black
tove shone orange through the open top, above it, on the
eiling, a smudgy halo. The floor was raw wood with pools
of braided rugs. A chest at one end served also as a bench;
a heavy bed-rug lay folded on it. On the sides, toward the
other end were bunks; two more above were pulled up by
leavy leather straps. Inside was clean, busy, lived in; there
vere brightly covered pillows, soft extravagant quilts, scarfs,
shawls, necklaces on pegs on the walls, swinging slightly
vith the sway of the wagon in its ruts, settling deeper in.
There were candles scented with pine oils or bayberry in-
ense, sprigs of herbs hung up, other odours seeping out of
small wooden boxes piled in a corner. The one window was
curtained on the inside. Outside the shutter tapped like the
peak of a bird on a hollow tree.

There was never anyone else in the shadows; only the
boy and Sibbi, warmth, silence and knowledge.

9

The children were completely unmanageable, as if they
already knew Christmas was the last holiday of the year,
before the long stagnant winter months claimed them, wore
them down gradually in cold, darkness and boredom. The
uneasy months when the sickly and old were watched
closely. It was them most of all that the chill affected, as if

113

their bones responded only to the sun, not imitations. Th
months when the latitudes were surely northern, when th
sun appeared now and again, far away, like the pale flag o
a foreign country on the horizon, while the North and th
Night ranged all around.

Mending was put away in sewing baskets and the to
was let fall shut until after Twelfth Night. Pennies wer
drawn from tin boxes and old socks to buy the most mar
vellous presents in the general store. There were deliverie
from the mail-order catalogues. The man and his childre
went up the Country Path inland to cut the plumpest o
tallest or best tree for their parlour. Popping corn, cran
berries and candles were sold out. The stores were empty
the houses full.

The children left. There was a shocking swamp of still
ness as if a curtain had fallen after the final act. It was good
being alone finally. Morgan sat and watched the smoke
from the fire rise up the chimney.

It snowed like secret the night through. With no soun
of wind. At dawn it stopped for a sunrise of red warning
then the thick dark cloud settled again and the snow con
tinued.

It was perfect; the most urgent activity was quelled, th
most responsible person quieted by the billows of soft ne
snow. Morgan roused a fire and set the kettle on the stove
Inside and out the air hung in a bleached half-light. He wa
used to the way holidays arranged themselves inside him
Sometimes he felt Christmas was an ornament, a fragile
faraway scene in an eggshell that he couldn't hold in his
hand. The snow was held in the world of a child's toy.

Christmas Eve the snow stopped just before bedtime and
the sky crinkled, it was so fresh with stars and a half-moon.
Morgan walked down into the village unseen. A village out
of memory; a picture-book landscape. The trees stilled by
snow. The light from the windows mellow, tempered fire

nd candle flame. The snow was soft. Christmas morning
fter the dark cold had lain on it, it would have a skin. Per-
aps the children would misinterpret his footprints.

Snow clung to the houses as a web holds a fly. He was
hinking. What happens when one lives so close to the sea,
vhen the land is barely under the elbow?

The landwash: being between the forces. Earth, stone
nd sea beneath your boots. One step out and you're driven
nto doing or drown; one step back and your element earth
s there for work, play, safety; but right there, at the edge,
ou're lulled, stunned. Right there at the edge of the sea is
he pulse, the heartbeat.

He heard the cat-ice slough away from the shore and was
urprised to find himself that close to the edge.

The lean lull at the edge of the new year. The time of the
ear when the Norsemen had rolled the wheel of fire,
wined with straw, from hilltop down to the winter sea. A
ew thin moments, elusive, foam on the black fluke of a
whale gone back to sea. The year sounded. It left a slick that
shone. It seemed late in the day to be remembering morning
dreams. Looking forward into another country, forward.

The bird called in the dark, echoing for landfall, for the
bottom of the sky. The bird having survived the deaths of
last year—the wake, watchful; the wail and the singing
intertwined. He had always thought of the dawn as pure,
having been filtered across the sea. What chance did a new
year have? It was not in the nature of a stone to stop. It was
the need of man to reconnoitre. He clung to the hinge, the
nadir of the season. Consciously re-organizing any cells that
might have gone astray. Morgan was breathing air that had
been through it countless times. After all, everyone was
here. The pulse of truth was in everyone's throat. He was a
lake fed by overhead rains and underground springs: the
careless woman—she was there, down under the summer
bush off the Country Path; the postman—beggerman be-

neath his rags, beneath the desperate rosy cheeks of rum the thief with fishes's fins sticking out of his cheeks, falling out of his pantleg; the rich man; the chief—suede patches on his elbows.

Morgan in turn fed many rivers. Saw some of himself flowing outward. He watched pieces of himself going on but it seemed he could never be with a single person, always

When he wanted to confess there was no-one. No-one he wanted to talk to; no-one he trusted. This was of his own making, learned from his own experience.

To call this time coming a new year was wrong, Morgan thought; it felt so ancient. An ice fog climbed out of the sea; winter-drab birds hunched against the cold, exposed and isolated.

He went out for his walk. By the time he got to town he couldn't see his feet. Chances were it would clear a little when the night wind came from farther out at sea, so he went into the tavern. Warm, brown, rowdy. The burden of smoke was everywhere. Smoke in layers between the cheese and ham sandwiches. Morgan was really too tired to join. He sat at the edge; drank and ate and watched. Behind him the noise of song, mottled conversation and abrupt laughter. Periodically he looked out the window to see if the fog had lifted. Figures moved in the window-glass. The evening became timeless; when the fog finally lifted into the clouds it was late.

The wind blew steadily now from the sea and his body like a sailor's mizzen, the small flag-sail on the back of the fishing-boats, kept him going straight. The clouds began moving in his head. Why, why must they begin again, just when it all seemed most plain. He was stumbling into painful territory. He was clumsy. He had avoided this landfall whenever possible. This time, however, it was not a matter of choice. The fibre of his mind spun out.

And when he slept, he dreamed. He gathered the sheet

where it was folded over the blanket into his fingers and held on. So he could come back from the places his dreams took him; places he dared not go in the waking day.

He was waiting. Waiting made him feel he shouldn't be where he was, as if he hadn't moved on to the next occasion.

He watched. Where he had been in his life was receding into time, out from his centre into his past. Lava flowing, falling out into cold space where it would slow down so he could see it.

It looked like stone: the light moved around and made it seem one shape with several faces. There were rifts, edges, angles, swellings and a deep hollow. He wanted to run his hands over it, into it; down into that darkness, that mystery that was his own secret. But he couldn't reach all the way down. Perhaps here was danger, a nest of adders or worse; here could be emptiness beneath the cold smooth stone.

He couldn't see anything there; he couldn't reach or touch, there. When his breathing slowed he heard something. An early sound, with an echo around it. He listened; he didn't know what was happening. Only this primitive sound. He found himself wondering if the cry wanted to be heard at all, or overheard. Then he began to hear words in the wailing. He could do nothing but listen. . . .

"Don't, please don't, no, no, please don't, no, no, no, please. . . ." And the voice broke off into helpless sobbing.

It was terrible; he didn't want to hear it. Why did he have to listen to that disembodied voice?

He couldn't see; he couldn't touch. A smell came up out of the stone a smell of cold, sweat and sickness. And despair, to which in his helpless dream he felt a right. He wasn't one of those who are betrayed from outside. If he was to be destroyed, it would be from within.

But the odour, the cold dry stone, the damp sobbing voice; these shapes showed in his dreams where there was no help.

When all the land and almost everyone in it was asleep Sibbi woke up. The only thing she could feel was her breathing. It dominated her whole being. It was the only link she still had with life. It took every effort, every fibre. Her lung pressed on her ribs. Why had it been so painful? Her rib had hurt so much at first. What did that mean, *first*? Before the thought got further a white blind was drawn. She made an uneasy transition into the brown-grey celibacy of night lit only by the white flame of the oil. She got up though it was chilly, for often there was no feeling on her skin.

Morgan heard her coming across the floor and got up. He saw a pale skimpy girl, feathery greyish hair, sunless skin and downturned eyelids. Her body was lost in faded flannel, save for the two points of her breasts. Her hands were behind the nightdress, but her feet stuck out like icicles frozen on the brown floor. He caught her eyes open.

They were trying to follow and find Morgan. But instead she felt the signs, the rituals of touch that happened when his shape came round her. His hand enclosing her chin, lifting her face; his other hand across her shoulder, the pressure leading her. It was solid and deliberate. The weight of Morgan's hand on her neck was good. Thus she listened until the nighthawk flew its dark skyways through her brain, making her listen to its howl, and she lost her place on the outside paths.

When he touched her, her limbs went rigid; and when he turned up the light he saw that her eyeballs were dry. He shut her eyelids. He massaged her arms and shoulders. Her skin was the colour of the snow-blue light of dawn. He rubbed more vigorously. Her heart was beating and there was breath. Why was the rest of her cold and dry like death? Where had she gone; why couldn't he follow? He was lonely and afraid.

He took her straw-blond head in his hands, caressed her cheeks with his thumbs. Each time it began as if he were

118

uching a stranger and the stranger in himself.

He put her into her own narrow bed under the window. There were voices, or perhaps it was the last whisperings of he fire. Light and shadow swooped around the room like a rantic bird, then was gone. She felt the weight of covers nd a touch on her forehead. With her face turned to the vindow she saw the moon-listening alders in the dark night.

He stirred up the ashes. The wind bruised itself on stone valls and windows. Not welcome. He fixed tea. It was well ast midnight. He sat Sibbi upright to spoon-feed her with ea and honey and milk. She swallowed the warm drink utomatically. Morgan held her while he drank his own. When he was done he put the cup on the floor. Turning her ound, she lay in his arms. He didn't feel like a whole per-on.

This ancient place. The bone-splintering loneliness of his hildhood came back to him. Instead of the wood-smell of he fire the prevailing odour was the wet cold of the stone. He turned the lamp out; the shadows softened.

Day after tomorrow the children would be back. He held onto that. Evergreen children. They had as little memory as he did. He longed for their immediacy. When he was with hem each moment was entire, exacting, demanding.

The fire was silent. The stones were sweating and the clock beat. At that moment he held more tightly to the only living thing in his world.

And it was only January.

10

How far had she grown? She climbed out of the hollow between the hills. She came up out of the sea glowing with phosphorus. The barbed wire she lived behind was cut and rolled up. She surrendered, as the northern lights glimmer and grow, then surrender to the sun, to be reborn again and again, each time more brilliant, incandescent, ethereal. She developed a centre of gravity and it moved back and forth from her head to her womb. A secret lay hidden in her flesh. Her person, nearly extinguished, was alive again.

Sibbi tried to reach Jason out of this reserve of warmth, but the wind was too vigorous. It blew her hand this way and that.

She had never cried before, but she knew how to do it at night. Jason slept on top of her tears. Having experienced a kind of companionship she was now still more alone. Untouched by blood, a thin windy boy had bruised her.

The ritual of surviving the ice was rigorous. She and Jason didn't speak. Their humours circled round each other. Jason sat at the table with his hands laid on the wood, apart from the rest of him, with nothing to do. The veins on his wrists and his hands were blue and bold. Freezing from inside, slowly. Once he'd had a core, something alive and pliable; now little by little, he was hardening.

He was cold but didn't seem to feel it. When he came in from his chores he left the door open. He'd lost his scarf in the snow and his coat was open at the throat. When Sibbi went up to him and put her hand to his neck his skin was wet and cold.

He left the cabin in the morning darkness and didn't come back until it was dark again. When he entered, the night stood at the door, a silent, solid wall.

He let the fire be, but blew out the lamps and snuffed the candles. Sibbi knew instantly when he was there because the shadows moved. Holes opened. Bleak hollows, sunk in the dark. It made her anxious. Where before Jason had sat in front of the fire on the edge of the bench she now sat alone, her elbow on the table. Jason stayed back in the shadows. Gone into the corner to take off trousers and boots. He wrapped the cold, black night round himself and got

nto bed. The dog poked his nose under Sibbi's hand in her
ap. He breathed louder than Jason. Sibbi didn't even turn
o see if he was there.

Later the dog lay down for the night in his place by the
warm hearthstone, so Sibbi was left alone. She moved her
hand into the fan of light from the fire. She didn't want to
go to sleep, nor to stay awake. To sleep was to lose touch
with peace, with memory, with sensation. In the night, with
the rhythmic fire, all things were possible. She was alone,
but whole. To sleep was to climb into a tomb next to someone who was dying. But she was healthy and young and she
was tired. To stay awake was to defy the new spirit within
her.

The days turned. Everything she did was done with a difference. Chores were done automatically, without thought.
In the midst of something she would find herself standing
stock still, a partially rinsed cup in her hand, a duster halfway across the shelf, feeling every pore breathing. She pol-
ished the bottom of a pan and looked at herself in the surface. There she was: a girl, a friend, a lover. There were her
eyes, blue pieces of summer sky. Her skin pale. Her hair,
yellow wheat. She was careless and enchanted.

Spring came early to her. Unknown birds migrated
through her, their wings reaping the wind, oscillating in
the incandescent light. She broke through the snow, thin,
weedy. She swelled up like a bud, the secret folded inside
her. The air was palpable, vivid, or hazy and mysterious.
Above all there was mystery in the winter light.

Jason saw the winter sky from his vice. He felt the weight
of it on his head. He put his hands up to push it away, but
it pressed harder and harder until he was forced to the
ground. His arms rigid, upstretched, held back the sky. His
eyes were open; he could see it. Panic ran in his bones. Then
his eyes shut and the star-crushed dark of the windy apple-
tree came back. Instead of snow it was grass, wild thyme

still open at the edges when all the flowers were closed fo the night. Green wood was growing inside the apple tre He'd had a special arrangement, then, with growing thing: Green and tender. Seeds learning their lessons under th ground among stones and worms, above the ground be tween the sun and the rain. Jason lay close on the ground dug his fingers down among the roots. The sky was sof velvet.

When he opened his eyes again the cold stole up his nos trils. The slate of sky closed its teeth, became solid, benign indifferent. His hands were numb in the snow. He got up motioned with his axe and went after another tree.

One day when the wind was March, the ground sloughy Sibbi put her scarf and coat on to go to school. She wante to hear some words spoken. She remembered the teacher' voice. She remembered a poem when she didn't know wha a poem was. With the vast blue at his back, he had looke at her until she felt shy, read to her until she felt shy in he soul. The years had intervened, interfered, and now she wa crying for everything lost and everything gained.

The mist wound itself in a coil around the great dar trees and engulfed them. It lay in edgeless pools, sank int the moss abruptly. It threaded the needles on the evergreen: and spun clouds on their branches. The earth was thawing gently. The ground and its mosses, the rocks and thei lichen, drinking the sun-melted ice, were again emerging from their frost-bleached colours. Speaking to the milky blueing sky. Sibbi ran her hands over her body. It was thin the bones stuck out, there were hollows, but under he hands she felt a certain weight, a heaviness. She remem bered sitting on the lap of a faceless woman, nestling, lean ing into the softness of her body. Now her own body, this spring, was becoming like that.

The double door into the school was always a difficul threshold to cross. She was wary as an animal not among ts own kind. Only she was what was new.

Inside was a grey cave. Mute maps curled their corners inward. Chalk dust lay like pollen. The children were seated, spaced regularly like furrows. All their heads turned when he was halfway in, flowers toward the light. Not until the teacher had called them back was she able to enter and sit in her place apart at the back of the room. She looked up to the front, over the heads of the children.

Parts of her were uneasy: her eyes, her shoulders, tense, stiff. The smell of bodies was thick, steam rose from damp jackets and scarves. Feet shuffled, scuffed. A word from someone, a cough, a sniffle, a sneeze, a whisper, a reprimand. Sound circled like a bird in a fog looking for a place to light. She closed her eyes, spread her hands on the desk. Her fingers found the pencil. She picked it up, opened her eyes to the scribbler, there too. With that much assurance, she began to gather the sounds and smells and sights together. She turned the scribbler. Its pages were loose because she had pulled out so many. She drew the swellings of her body, the musky odour of the children, the steel-in-syrup voice of the teacher, the rough plaster of the walls. The safe and steady parts of her, her neck which was proud, her hips, sullen; these things sustained her in the daylight. She considered this place, its inhabitants. She considered the teacher who was also a man, now that she knew something concerning man. He was nervous, his brow knit. He had added weight and shadows to his face. Lines from loneliness, wrinkles from thinking, from talking and laughing. It was an open face, human, used, revealed. All this to Sibbi to whom more was revealed by a leaf turning over in the rain than her own kin.

It was in the eyes. His eyes were open. She saw that suddenly. This was what was wrong with Jason. How long had it been since she had seen his eyes? Since he had been hurt? He had known with her then, in fever and fear. Was that the last time? When the sun went under the earth, Jason' eyes had gone into the winter darkness. She couldn't remem ber what colour they were. Where his eyes had been there were now hooded sockets under the jutting bones of his brow.

She came up out of her thoughts into the explosion of the teacher's presence. Who was he to appear out of the grey stones at nine in the morning, to govern in this realm until three in the afternoon and then disappear again? And who was that other man who waved when he saw her up in the hills? Or the man who ages ago had met her in the strange starched bluff among the salted trees?

What would happen to her when the sun set?

On another day when the wind was cold but the sun was rising with the spring, she went in search of that man. Her shadow ran over the long edge of the bluff beside her. Every thing was still. The land had changed little but it wasn't the same. She had come with too little. She had nothing to eat. No blanket to sit on. She had no book to read. She sat against one of the trees, put her hands over her head to hold onto the smooth petrified trunk. She sat and watched the day unfold; then when day was well established, the magic gone out of it, the hope of magic gone out of it, she went home.

When spring spilled the children out into the soggy schoolyard for recess, Sibbi watched from the hill. She sat between the thin, grey-green bushes, perfectly camouflaged, and watched. But she wasn't remembering. Sometimes she dreamed of the school children playing. The grass was beaten into the dust. Before they came out the yard was bare, waiting. She was in the wind then, wandering over the empty ground which was waiting for the children and their games. Then they came. She watched and came closer. The children smiled at her shyly. They touched the ends of her fingers. They tapped on her toes. They took her hands nd pulled her into the circle of their dance. She was safe. n the dream. But in the daylight these things had never happened. She didn't know what a best friend was. She'd never gone to another child with a secret. Her secrets were entrusted to the silence of a flower, but the petals fell off before the secret was forgotten. So she told it to the stump of a tree, but it was dead. There were other listeners: a corn-husk doll, a shrivelled apple face, the old horse, the puppy until he grew up, her own reflection in a pond or shiny pan. Finally she had buried her face in the soft, strong flank of the pony.

One of the sheep scrambled under the fence-rails and wandered off into the deep snow that still lay in the valley. The sediment of Jason's anger was stirred and when he found the sheep among the budding trees he hacked its skull open with his axe. Its blood ran all over the snow.

Jason was having trouble with his stars. They wouldn't stay in place, they burned, consumed themselves, exploded, leaving black holes in his mind. When he looked up for their guidance, a ship lost on the bleak moving night, they were gone. He was frightened.

Spring was hard coming. The winds were rough with the returning birds, tearing their nests apart. It was raw and chill. It rained for too many days. Leaves were close-furled; the seeds stayed underground. The season fought with polar winds and rising sun.

Jason was stiff when the lambs were born in May. The ewes were uneasy when he came among them, handled their newborn. Several refused to accept their young. He had to take them into the cabin, milk the fractious ewes and feed the weakening lambs. Even so, with Sibbi silently helping, many were lost. The little dead bodies were laid outside one by one. Sibbi's heart, so gentled by this spring, was hurt by all this unseasonable dying.

She fled as soon as she could. Fled into the sweet, unde-

manding silence she found under the curved caravan roof.
She could think of no other way to ease her feelings than
in the dark where she was seen more clearly. When she
stood in front of Jason he didn't see her. When she stood
in front of the teacher, it was not the right time. There was
a crowd.

A night, a day, and then another night. The bodies of the
lambs were cold and unnatural, laid out in regular rows.
On the dark ground they were still-white, reflecting the full
moon. Waves were breaking on the distant shore; the lambs
were a broken, frozen wave. The night was without depth.
The trees were black paper cut-outs. When a nighthawk
cried out of sequence its voice jarred with the cries of the
lambs. Every sound froze in her ears. The ground was crisp
with late frost; each step crackled like fire, was printed in
her head.

She stopped for a moment at the top of the hill, but she
hadn't gone far enough. The animals watched her. She was
cold. She crouched down, afraid, hiding her face in her
hands, trying to find a place to hide. Some place where she
wasn't put off, forbidden. Some place where she could
understand the rules.

The more she opened herself, showed herself above
ground, the less strong were her roots. She was presented
naked to the weathers of these people who had caught her
—whom she had let catch her. Which was it? She couldn't
tell. In the sunlight she couldn't be sure. They could see her
shadow, a betrayal. All of her was above ground. She
couldn't dig into the still-wintered crust of the earth with
her hands. She could only go on. There were too many
things she didn't know. Seeds of expectation had been
planted. She couldn't always cry alone, watch the rivers run
down, listen to the desolate foghorn, know the seasons on
her skin. Not all those things alone. She went on, broke out
of the trees into the camp in the valley. All the way, won-

lering. Wondering what was happening.

Jason didn't have to see a thing to know it. He simply lug into the underground of his mind. He appeared in the village with a cart of dead lambs and wool from the spring shearing with a red cloth tied around his forehead as if he was in pain. He didn't haggle at all over the price of the wool. People stood around, uneasily, memorizing shapes: cart, pony, dog, girl. When his business was done, Jason remained standing. It wasn't until one of the men made a move to shelve the woollen bundles that Jason spoke about the gypsy encampment. He was dissatisfied with the answers to his questions. No word of when they would move on.

Jason had bought a wide-brimmed black hat. Now that the sun was full in the northern sky he needed protection when he went into the summer meadows with the sheep. All the things he didn't want to think about, yesterday and today, were present under the hat. All the things that stung him. There, in the shadowed glades and soft hills, the hawk circled leisurely above him. The hawk was curious. In the night the moon was curious.

He couldn't read the maps in the sky any more. He demanded that the earth right itself, stand still for a day, a moment, but it ignored him. He woke in the middle of the night and tried to take the sheep out to pasture. He was so feverish he lay fully clothed in the icy stream. When he went to command the dog to bring in the herd, the words stuck in his throat.

One night in midsummer when all the forces of the earth and sky were pulling against each other, Jason broke apart. The hawk slanted out of the sky and struck its talons through his head and heart. There was no escape; he was almost relieved. He would fight but he would lose. The hawk would carry him off. But he fought, he fought by destroying everything he would have to leave behind.

The days of the new year were counted out. Lived in the dark of winter hours and snow. In the small semicircle of absolute duty. Simply to survive took a great deal of effort. The seas rose high in the harbour. When Morgan stood on the shore the ocean was sighting for a new level in the hills.

The children were back. With their pale blunt eyes.

At nine they came in the dreary cold dawn, hot baked potatoes in their pockets for their hands. And the light was draining away behind the hills when they trudged home. They were so small in the landscape. It would snow again. The children would come again. The slow climb of a thought, wearying: Where? Would he be going on like this forever?

The sun was cold in the sky from clean snow and roving wind. That white sun, its flames burning with ice.

Sibbi pressed her forehead on the curtain, then on the cold window-glass. She heard nothing. She couldn't hear the fire unless she turned around and looked at it. She saw Morgan outside, a red scarf bobbing in the air, going away. She drew back. The pulse in her throat broke around the breath that was caught there. Blood bathed the back of her eyes, seeped through her insides. The pain startled her, but the nether world wouldn't come. The blood beat like a tide against her skull. Her hands went to her ears, she heard herself moaning when the pain broke on her bone. She ripped the curtain from its hook. No escape. Blind, she ran outside, out from under the shadow of the house into sun-light. Still blind. She sank onto her hands and knees, bending forward until her face lay in the snow. For a moment there was nothing. Then, with the snow burning on her skin, the thread frayed enough for her to tell the difference. The red was turning green. And she was cold. She remembered what it was like to be cold and this was the same. This

as cold sun, snow, ice, dry wind. This was winter. She felt
he overwhelming silence of the snowfield and the hill.

She ran back inside. It was warm and dark. She ran
hrough the schoolroom, threw open the door. The wind
eemed blue from the sea. The brilliance of the water star-
led her. She was shivering again. She could hear the grind-
ng sound as the tide swept through the granite rocks of
he shore. She shut the door and the sound stopped. She
reathed steadily.

She put on boots, her coat and scarf. She pulled the back
door shut behind her. This was winter. The light on the
now was the light of an early world.

She stepped away from the sea. Where the sea sand deep
beneath stopped against stone, the land was less ravaged by
ea salt and sea wind. The trees grew thick as cushions. The
ound of creaking tree limbs, the soft thud of snow slipping
off the branches, making prints on the smooth drift. Pools
of weak sun between blue-tree shadowed ground.

Sibbi got over the top of the hill, broke through the trees
and came upon the cabin, which had become part of the
snowscape. The door was held open by snow. The light
inside was stretched thin, not enough of it to fill the space.
A fox, amazed by the intrusion, ran out.

Morgan came up behind her. But he couldn't reach. He
stuck in the doorway. He saw her body: the posture of a
broken pitchfork. He saw her eyes go black. The whole
place felt like cold blood to him. He didn't like being in
places built by man when no man remained; it was like
facing his own mortality.

Sibbi took her hands off the wall, gathered her collar in
her fingers. In the middle of the floor she turned around,
once. Her fingers traced the seams of her coat. Sometimes
she turned suddenly as if she heard a dog scratching or some
unknown sound.

She went toward the window. The bed was in the way.

Her hands fluttered over it. The cold was in her flesh, lik
lice. She put her knee on the bed, making sure it was covere
by her coat. She took the flowerpot from the windowsi.
and threw it on the floor. She took the dirt and dry roots an
crumbled them in her hands. To dust. Then Morgan presse
upon her, lifting her, but she collapsed and he had to carr
her down the hill. The winter in her had not run its course.

The next season the boats went out for lobster. They rod
the great waves, rising up on the crests until the propeller
sliced the air, then slid out of sight into the wide, dee]
trough. Men were lost to the sea and men were saved. O
the two, the churchyard and the sea, the sea had claimed
many more lives; stones over empty graves testified to old
men and young lost at sea.

But spring oozed out of the southern lands, catching a
seed here and there that grew up green in the snow. There
was a blue sleep of fog across the horizon between the sea
and sky, slanting between wind and water. The voices o.
the children came back like snowfleas come out on the snow
Fierce, alive. The vital instinct to be born, to become, ar
rived with the undercurrents of spring. Frost in the ruts wa
broken by the childrens' boots. Cobwebs were spread out
like split cod and rib bones. In the morning the children
ran through them.

Everything was gathered together in spring. All the raw
gaps, the scars, the skeletons, were buried as the green
things grew toward each other over the stones. Weeds grew
in the eroded wagon-ruts between dawns, and next day their
seeds sprang into the wind. The day after, the trucks
squashed them flat. The bluff was like a green-gold lid over
the blue eye of the sea.

There was a ritual lull between the lobster trapping and
the running of the fish on the shelf. Where the cove bent,
a hook stretched out to sea, a new boat was being readied

or launching. They had to wait until the spring tide ran in under the slip.

The smell of oakum was heavy in the morning fog. Women with the arms of their sweaters tied around their necks leaned on the fence-rails looking out to sea now and again, then back to each other, to exchange the morning's news. On their hips, monkey-straddled, their babies. Beneath their feet the toddlers. The men stood on locked knees, one hand lost in overall pockets, the other gripping a suspender as if it were a line, or cuddling the bowl of a glowing pipe. Some walked about, pointing, commenting. Old men, shrunk inside their collars. Old wise sea-men with their eyes burned iceberg blue.

The tide swelled up under the ramp, lapping like a tame green dragon, inviting. The boat was unleashed and christened. It slid away hesitantly, to tumultous cheers.

By the time the fish were running the boats were ready.

When Sibbi broke out of the more remote regions it was a secret.

She was able to harbour her thoughts, thoughts that herded like deer on their winter feeding grounds. One day snow in a dry flurry, aimless, diffuse, the season undecided. The next day, the snow clinging to everything in the new light.

As if her dreams were finally making sense, for several weeks she slept a great deal.

She lay in a dark cold hollow. She knew about the snow-sky, opaque, light underneath with its belly full of hoar-frost, dark on top. The last time she had looked it was a time of ice and snow. She had no reason to believe this would change soon. It was enough that she cared about the world outside.

She lay in her cocoon all alone. She didn't touch the sides or the top. It was black, dark as the abyss. When she noticed she felt that the air she breathed was cool, but had no smell. The sea woke under the ice and explored in melted circles.

The weight of a single drop of water on the back of her hand. She began to feel prints as her skin began to thaw.

She lay in her cell. The wind beating against stone. The storm was in her dream. The wind, unseen, blew in her ear and kept her blood tied to the sea rhythms. She took soundings in the hollows of her mind and began to carve an image, an idea there. It gave her a new dedication to herself.

When she woke in the light she saw Morgan. She knew who he was; an easy and comfortable memory. She saw Morgan moving to and fro, as if in a dream.

She lay still as a tree root and felt she showed. She wanted to be hidden for a while. She was tired. The dreams were in her bones.

Daytime invested her senses. She needed time to get used to it.

It was very early. Morgan was held in the drift of his dreams, a time of grace and mercy. His skin wasn't awake yet; he felt a light chill on its surface. His dreams trembled. Time and rising light began to intercede. To organize.

With morning came urgency and restlessness. Morgan assumed, as he did every spring, that all the secret intentions would be realized. This year he needed something new; he was impatient. Things were too tight, too restrictive. This merry-go-round needed more time than he had. Wearily he pushed the hair back out of his eyes.

Morgan went walking the lengths of the shore where all things were possible and nothing real. When he came back he took Sibbi by the hand and went walking again. She was very careful. She never tripped over stones, the long grasses never snagged her legs. He noticed that she was drawn by the ebb tide; drifting closer and closer to the receding sea. Once he let her go. She walked toward the sea without looking aside, though the hand he had held remained behind her, stretched backward toward him. This broken wing didn't upset her balance. When the water washed around er legs she stopped. Looking down, she bent to put one free hand into the water. He didn't move to come up behind her. She went farther, scooping up handfuls of water, throwing it back into the sea. Then stood with her arms straight up, the water over her. Morgan saw the timid line of the horizon between her fingers.

"That's right," he whispered as she beckoned toward the lighter part of the sky. She turned her hand this way and that. She looked at it. Then she clenched her fists to her chest, her arms tight to her sides, her head down. Morgan started, then stopped. He didn't know what to do. He looked at her back, shaking through the dove-coloured coat. She was crying, sobbing, all pulled together, not scattered by her fear. She was separate and he didn't know what to do.

She stopped just as suddenly. Cold, stunned. The grey water sucked the sand from beneath her feet. She was about to be swallowed like a pebble.

"She mustn't drown," he thought, and started toward her. Before she knew he was near she turned. Her mouth was open, smiling: gentle, real, connecting. And her eyes were open. She was looking for someone. He wondered what she had found behind the tears, beyond the horizon. She looked down at their hands. Then she moved her hand toward his, lightly, not quite committed. When she had gone as far as she could, Morgan slid his fingers around hers. She shook away, then reached again toward him, looked into his face. He put his hand under hers, gently, as if it were a fragile bird. But it was quite steady, offered as a solid thing, a story. He covered her hand with his.

The pale sky and the bright pebbles among the bones. He had her hand in his. He said:

"You're not afraid. . . . When you're ready. . . finally. . . if you can."

He thought perhaps he'd been too sure she was looking at him.

133

ISBN 0 88750 205 9 (hardcover)
ISBN 0 88750 206 7 (softcover)

Edited by Sally Eaton and designed by Michael Macklen
Cover by Rudi Haas.

Printed in Canada

PUBLISHED IN CANADA BY OBERON PRESS